My Name is...
Paul Belardo

by

T. J. Samson

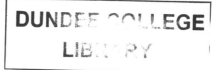

Published by New Generation Publishing in 2013

Copyright © Thomas J. Samson 2013

First Edition

www.newgeneration-publishing.com

 New Generation **Publishing**

Dedicated to Paul and those who know…

1

…that's stupid. No, it's more like a frame. Inside it I'm logical. There is a storm around it. The clouds don't move. Sounds good. I can hear myself introducing the idea soon as my representation of this 'inner blackness'. He'll like that. He's always asking me to describe it.

He warbles like an old video though. But medical bits make it through above the rumble of people carriers outside. I can hear him now. He says it's vital that I understand the consequences of agreeing to this new medical trial. *Right*.

My cousin Ian always talks about the consequences of 'doing nothing'. He'll be cleaning his pet shop floor, brushing away a porridge of piss, oats and hair. If I was there he'd put the kettle on, reach up for chocolate digestives, talk about how he'll 'act to realise his dreams' by selling up and opening another shop in Brighton. His face lights with futures.

Jan says she doesn't have a future yet. She's stuck being a chemist in Fairfields, a council scheme in north Curby. The chemist's is next to a post office and Jan detests her job and her husband; he's a boring bastard, a political type, a diplomat. Jan will be thinking of leaving him for me while methadone disappears down the throat of her last customer. Addicts are getting older, she'd say. Some are in their fifties. Her husband's fifty, abroad mostly. She'll probably phone me soon. We've arranged to meet after this appointment.

Yes, I'm listening. I understand. I must comprehend the

possible impact of the drug's effects. I must be methodical when recording my feelings. He says it's a *central* part of the research, uses his terminologies to show he regards me as being intellectual. I like it.

Curtains are vital too, though. I remember orange ones. Sunshine soaked through them, in childhood rooms dyed and still. In this room there's only fawn: a meaningless colour. The carpet's related: a dull tan. And desk, chair: council brown. And this practice's in a colourless village. Well, it used to be a village anyway. Still called 'Upton Mews' though, still far enough from Curby to feel elite. They cling to names here.

Dead colours magnetise you down though. Doctor must know so why doesn't he redecorate, move? Not very professional, is it? Dullness seeps into muscles. Gives you cramps, bleeds black inside the skull. He knows this. Everything's related. Cause and effect: fawn to black. And me, knowing this, glued inside myself. See, it's important to think of colour. But the doctor doesn't.

So the drug's been developed to have a profound effect. Yes I'm listening doctor. He always doubts me. Of course Lithium is superior to placebo. It was successful in crossover trials. So the result of this development is a new mood stabiliser. Hold on: mood stabilisers aren't *new*. Aren't you meant to offer combinations anyway, like Olanzapine, Valproate, or an anti-psychotic? Check your prescribing guidelines doctor, come on.

'Yes, ah, doctor, a new mood stabiliser does not constitute a development.'

Okay, I'm absolutely right: mood stabilisers are *not* new. However, this drug may effectively kill off the depressive episodes. So he's a murderer then. Well they all are. Why kill it though? Can't we play with it first? I say too much. I've condemned it now. If I complain, he'll know I'm its accomplice.

I killed a hamster last month, been out jogging around Curby city centre, bouncing off cobbles in pedestrian areas. Jan's idea: exercise helps you sleep, calms you down. But when I ran, I lost myself. Three rushes of happiness after bounding past The Body Shop and I forgot who I was, where I lived, where I was. Didn't pay attention to the path.

Sprinted past a vet's. Collided with a kid holding a cage outside the entrance. A hamster was crushed, I fell onto the cage. It folded under me.

I apologised, took out the bloody hamster. The kid bawled; his mum appeared. She screamed. I explained that exercise could have a calming effect. She slapped me. I ran away and remembered my name was Paul Belardo.

Yes, I understand, the drug's a new derivative of Lithium. Its potency has been honed to rid me of depressive episodes. The wonder drug, so easy, was successful in comparative trials. Yes, I remember, my first handout, the doctor's a teacher, see. And he's sensing a victory for medicine. You can tell. His face looks less plastic.

But why listen to this? This isn't you. You know that. I should tell him to...No, stop. No, really. *Come on*. Behave. Great, where do I sign then? But wait. Things to ask though, like how long will it take? What're the side effects?

'Ah, doctor, what is the duration of treatment before the drug engenders a change and are there significant psychological or physical ramifications?'

He's already told me? Really? But he'll repeat it to make sure I understand. I can hear his voice click onto rewind now. He says the drug may trigger mild psychosis, after weeks of treatment, without emphasis. But that's dangerous, isn't it?

'Doctor, this sounds precarious.'

Ah, of course, he'll prescribe other medications to counteract such a drastic reaction. In tests in America only 12% suffered such symptoms. Ok*ay*. Not an attractive statistic. He should work on his approach. Bleep out the variables. Numbers are hard. Stories are better. Tell me a story doctor. Come *on*! Wait…shuttup…I haven't had a depressive dip for months. Do I *need* this?

'Doctor, I'm aware that I haven't suffered from any significant episodes of depression for some time. Is this treatment necessary?'

Severe depressions will recur. I know they will, one's waiting, like a weather front in the North Atlantic, but I can't be bothered talking about it. Anyway it sounds so straight when he says it like that, *severe depressions.* I prefer other words.

When I told my cousin Ian about their diagnosis he laughed and said 'is that what they're calling it now?' His pet shop's down at Curby docks, south of the city centre, between a hairdresser's and bookmaker's. It looks out onto the new Compton Road Bridge which has plenty of sky above it. But that day was low and grey and the bridge led to nothing.

He was smiling when he said it; from a collection that mean different things. This one meant superiority: you could tell by the way it rose at the left, the eye above sharpened beneath his thick grey hair. And I like Ian's tan. It's his palette against the British monotone. I called it 'a marker of his drive against complacency' but he laughed then said 'you're naturally melancholic, that's what you are Paul. You always have been, simple as that. Don't give up on yourself.' I prefer melancholy to disorder. Disorder makes me feel guilty. Don't know why.

I feel guilty about existing.

Yes doctor, I understand the undertaking involved. You'll prescribe; I'll record my feelings. After that, the treatment will be reviewed.

Okay, these are the pills; I take them for three months. Got it. I come back and see you next week. Got it! Yes of *course* I've comprehended this fully. Let me sign. Let me *leave*. Thank fuck! Now, where did I say I'd meet Jan?

2

'Yeah, I'm just around the corner Jan. I know the doctor's is only minutes away. Well, I wanted some time. I'll be in the pub soon. Yes, I remember the plan. I have to go; it's foggy. I know, fog in summer, even in Upton Mews, awful. See you in five.'

Got this mobile free. See what you get for working for a charity called 'Curby Health Promotion' in the afternoons? They want me to be contactable. That's all. God knows why. Probably to seem modern. I'm only phoned and asked where I am occasionally, that's it.

I work at Curby University Library in the mornings. They don't give me phones but I have a free library membership.

Frank's my team leader at Curby Health Promotions. He's always asking how I am. Should he do that? Shouldn't have written anything under 'conditions' on the application form. Lesson learnt. Christine at the library would never be so repetitive.

Last week Frank asked if I could research on the connection between poverty and poor health. His face flattens when he talks. Like his brown hair. It's squashed into his head with gel. Maybe he wants others to think he denies his hair. So it looks like he won't be distracted from his role. His nose is flat enough to ignore; he's thin enough to seem dedicated.

Didn't work after his request though: too many thoughts. Like starving people wriggling in gutters, dead children in bushes, homeless families begging outside my home where vans full of food are parked (online delivery - it saves having to see people).

But so what? I cried in the toilet because I didn't care. That's when I knew an episode was due to roll in.

So I went out for a fag at the door and spoke to the disabled cleaner about poor housing in Fairfields. The area records the highest level of 'economic inactivity' in Curby, according to Frank. She said it was all Thatcher's fault, allowing people to buy their council homes in the eighties. I laughed, said I fancied Thatcher when I was young, had a poster on the wall and I said I would show her my Thatcher tattoo when she threw away her rolled cigarette, went in, started mopping.

The housing here in Upton Mews is frustrating, though. A few streets of cottages linked like a stone bus driven into pavement, going nowhere like everyone else on planet Earth. Fog dropping off low roofs again
and again, reminding all that nothing's new, never will be. I used to live in a rented cottage, in a lane behind this village. But let's not think about that.
　　This place used to be ignored, being two miles outside Curby, not far from the coast, Black Cliffs. Some still have thatched roofs, makes the mist seem ancient. Older people cower at newness in some houses but city families keep buying. Commuters have become conscious. And proud. No one's safe for long.
　　There are satellite dishes, a wine specialist, traffic, an Indian carry-out shop, CCTV cameras, mums and tots groups. I used to have coffee with Jan in the 'Parrot Café'. Now it's 'P. Dawn's Computer Maintenance and Digital Hire' with a yellow machine in the window that prints digital photographs. The fog's outside its door, trying to get in.

I walked out into a field of fog one night, behind Jan's house in a new development that crawls into countryside near here. Her husband had come home early from Brussels. I was forced into a sitcom reaction. Jan panicked, pushed me out the back door. I didn't laugh, but I should have. So I stood in the garden, watching her wash her hands in the sink, staring into the water. She didn't see me. She didn't move. I liked looking at her stillness and her husband didn't come into the kitchen.

I strolled into the fog, compelled to be lost. But in the mist it felt like I was inside some entity. A neuron in the brain of a god made of fog. I wanted to see its dreams!

I walked until I saw yellow lights. You get excited, could be anything. But it was only a new garage with a teenage boy in a glass cubicle listening to something on his Ipod earphones. I tried to run through the empty forecourt without him noticing, to deny it, but he saw me and screamed. I'm scary. Ruined the whole thing though! I could've hit someone.

Ah, here we are: the pub. It looks forced. It looked softer before. Name hasn't changed. People love names here: still the 'Upton Arms' but with space for more words. Maybe people here fear name change will deprive them of money. It used to be a room with a bar, pool table, juke box, peanuts, air of sedation. Now it has meals, plasma TV, aspirations, slit blinds. But I can peer through, see Jan sitting at a table reading. She's still wearing her lab coat under her duffle. No one else is in. She'll only meet me here at Upton Mews.

Should I drink though? Did he say anything about alcohol? Can't remember. Okay, go non-alcoholic. No repeats of last summer, god no. Ask the barman.

'Yeah, ah, can you advise me on your best non-alcoholic beverage? Coke? That'll do.'

Jan looks dazed. Probably work. Happens a lot. Sit

down beside her, look understanding then. Say something nice.

'Hey Jan. I had to get a coke, new meds. I hate that doctor's office. I mean, really, why have a practice in Upton Mews? Makes talking treatments seem so provincial. You can't take him seriously. Love your duffle coat though.'

'Why didn't you ask me if I'd like a drink?'

'You've got a drink; it's on the table, right there. What is it?'

'Pure vodka. Did you bring the menu? You haven't brought it.'

'No, shit, was I meant to…?'

'Doesn't matter. You were supposed to say things as well.'

'Was I?'

'You were supposed to ask me why I was on my own.'

'Oh. Did I forget anything else?'

'The whole plan. You should've sat beside me, demanded that I have a drink, rush off for the menu, come back and say you needed to eat to calm your desperate hunger, then you were going to call me a slut and slide your hand up under my skirt.'

'Can I still slide my hand under?'

'No, the mood's gone. You always do this. You've no imagination. So how was your day?'

Jan has a sloth's face, transplanted on in the late eighties, pioneer operation. Can see headlines, like…no, they've gone. But she still looks like a sloth, but taller, with long black hair in a very middle shade. She talks like a telephone sales type: here but ahead in time. Look, she's breathing, soft boobs bobbing, she's about to ask me if I'm a homeowner.

13

'So, what were you saying about new meds?'

'Yeah, I'm on another trial.'

'What are they called?'

'Can't remember.'

'Are they anti-psychotics, mood stabilizers, antidepressants?

'Mood stabilizers, new ones.'

'Let me see.'

She always rattles them before reading the label. Her face disappears into her hair when she stoops to read. Wonder if she'll reach for her reference book in her lab coat. She's sweating now, shining, with her two coats. Like a painted wall.

'Mmm, haven't heard of these before. Did the doctor mention side effects?'

'Psychosis, possibly severe, but the brief variety, perceived and already counteracted.'

'I hate it when you talk like that. Say something else.'

'The doctor advised, with a draconian register, spiritual fornication with a chemist.'

'One married to a diplomat?'

'It says so on the label, under 50 milligrams.'

'Finish your coke and get in the car.'

Jan's house now, eight miles from Upton Mews, hiding in the dark curve of a cul-de-sac behind tall hedges. Has a wooden balcony, looks American. I've never seen it in daylight. No sound here, no traffic drone. You walk up its drive and feel pagan. I leave at three in the morning and feel modern.

She never makes tea. The dining room is banned. I can sit in the guest bedroom. It's pastel, bare, feels made for waiting in and is painted every four months. I sit until she's showered. I'm only allowed to touch her feet until she orders me upwards. 40 minutes later I'm offered one glass of wine and have to smoke in the garden beside the greenhouse. I'm not to talk or make eye contact when I return, just leave.

But why isn't she in the shower yet? She looks like she's going to talk. No, return to the routine. Damn, she's opening her mouth, that wide slit.

'Paul, I want to leave him. What can you offer me?'

Again? She keeps asking…why does she ask this? Does she even know she's asking? She says it like she's not saying it, like she's speaking in a coma.

Other sloth-like women would never ask such questions. Christine wouldn't. But she's more fruit-like: a round orange face with red curls around it. You see ripples in her skin sometimes, and dimples, when she struts in her supervisory role at Curby University Library. Only work there five mornings a week and one Saturday a month. Last week, thought her face was going to burst, rind everywhere, when I placed a Coleridge biography amongst the works of Marx. But she would never bore me like this, she loves me too much…oh, better say something.

'No promises.'
    'Okay, I'll think about it. Now sit here while I shower and don't touch anything.'
    'Okay.'

The same reply, every time. Now she leaves the room. Her white coat sheds trailers in the kitchen. They're pink. Modern. Cool.

Oh, I can actually feel it, like cement in my head, but with something sparkling in the mortar. A quirky thing playing in there, tickling me like a child. Hope it's the meds.

3

'What time do you start in the library?'

'Forty - five minutes or so.'

'You at Health Promotion this afternoon as well?'

'Yeah.'

'You look tired Paul. Good job the library's close.'

'I feel ragged. Something's coming on.'

'I'll stick the kettle on.'

'Okay Ian.'

'I've no digestives. You're too early; I haven't been to the shops yet. You're a pain in the arse.'

'It's alright.'

Ian moves like someone on their way to take part in a fight to leave me here while he makes tea in the back room. Never liked sitting here alone. Too many eyes. Like that staring terrapin. Its yellow orbs throb like it knows something about me I don't. And they float, a little.

A woman's laughing in 'Curby Curls', the hairdresser's next door. Sounds cruel. And a puppy's yelping from inside a cardboard box with holes in it. Others join in. The cries of orphans. Poor Wendy. Kate was devastated. No, stop; it's going the wrong way. Think of anything. Like a dying bee...oh, he's back.

'Here's your tea Paul.'

'Cheers.'

'I got a brochure from Lipton Business Properties yesterday, from Brighton.'

'Great.'

'Look at this one with white pillars. I could call it *Brighton Pet Emporium.*'

'I like it.'

17

'There're no pet shops within two miles of it. I've done my research.'

'Sounds brilliant. So, selling up then?'

'Thinking about it, making plans. Nothing happens if you don't *act*.'

'I know.'

Every time he says 'act' his chin curls. But look at his eyes, so urgent, ready to roll into a taxi to Brighton. Why doesn't he follow them? Oh, his face's darkening a bit, even his grey hair. Demonic! Turn away, ignore it!

'You okay Paul?'

'Thought I was going to sneeze there!'

'You on another trial then?'

'Yeah.'

'Again? Everyone gets down Paul. Everyone feels great sometimes. That's life.'

'I know.'

'Yeah, so I've been discussing things with Mandy, showing her the brochures.'

'Is she keen?'

'Well, she's got Karl to think about. He's only fourteen. Exams next year.'

'Will you go without her then?'

Another smile from the collection. This one's straight. Don't know what it means.

I used to have a family like Ian's. Not now, not for years. Kate and Wendy. No, can't allow memory though, getting good at it.

Legs and arms are thickening with foreboding, slowing me. Fuck!

'So, another trial? What does Jan think of the new meds?'

'She's unsure this time.'

'I'd better organise the front shop. Relax for a bit, don't rush off.'

'Okay.'

He said he'd never wear an overall. Didn't want to look like a working class stereotype. But look, he's wearing a fawn one; he's brushing between boxes and cages. He doesn't realise.

But the shop window's turquoise: there's a curve of morning above Compton Bridge. Cars come towards us, over its bend, some with lights still on. Maybe they fear the day. Each light's a blue star. Better leave.

'Ian, I'd better go. I'm due at the library soon. I could do with some air before I start.'

'Okay Paul. But do me a favour.'

'What's that?'

'Stay off the tea. You look freaked.'

'Yeah, cheers.'

…drink the tea here then, before going in. Relax, breathe. That's better. It's cool, outside Curby University Library, shaded by knowledge. Love this campus, near the city centre yet immune to its commerciality. Full of pleasant students wearing second-hand clothes, chatting, drinking latte, eating orange wraps under trees outside old buildings.

This university was a Polytechnic eight years ago. It doesn't register in educational supplements. In 1853 it was a hospital built to cater for the injured from the Crimean War. Look at the façade, perfect neo-gothic: towers, arch windows, pointed arch doorway. Looks like a church, a 'church of the mind'. That's what

Christine calls it. She'll be waiting for me, to get the team meeting started. Wait though, eyes tired, probably red. Black shapes in the corners, gold spots. My disco orbs. I'll splash water on my face in the staff toilet.

Lights in here never change. Constant flicker. Like life in academic film. Sounds good that. Filming me on Floor One pushing books in metal cages but the trolley sticks on the carpet. I've told Christine, it creaks when you push. Students don't mind, depending on what floor you're on. I cause offence on Floor Three though, where they bring in laptops and get emotional.

Right, what's this? The Life of Robert Louis Stevenson?

Okay, Stevenson goes there. Thousands of works numbered to match a digital catalogue. Christine would be pleased with that description. Here she comes to check on me. She's a rectangle but looks round when she walks.

Why can't she confess her love for me, have an erotic fit in the reference section, rub journals over herself, her orange face juicy, calling for me? She loves me. She keeps putting her hand on my arm and leaving it there. Here she is.

'You missed the team meeting Paul.'

'Sorry Christine. Slept in. After I'm done here, where would you like me to go?'

'Is everything okay? You look exhausted.'

There it is: her hand on my arm. Hot and freckled. Looks like cereal. It suits her. Can see her eating breakfast alone at home: nothing exotic, apart from sliced banana, crunching through a fraction of a planned order. Her rust skirt and top are heavy, some bran-like material. She wants me to say something.

'I'm fine Christine.'

'Are you sure Paul?'

'Yeah, honestly, don't worry.'

'Okay. There's another pile for this section downstairs. I know you like this section.'

'Yeah.'

She's not looking at me but her hand's still there. Now it's glistening a little, around the nails. Oh thank god, it's gone.

'Will I see you at lunchtime in the Students' Union today?'

'Yeah, but I'm still not eating couscous.'

'Ha, okay Paul. Bye for now.'

'Yeah bye.'

Yeah…bye. Ho hum.

The Picture of Dorian Gray. Is this the copy I vandalised years ago? It's been mended. There're lumps of yellow glue on the spine. Could be the same book. What page did I graffiti? Here it is, that sentence stained with purple marker, on our capability for "infinite pity". Oscar knew. I showed this to the Doctor first time we met, to explain. To show him how I felt about myself. Better than my words. I've offered him lots of lines. Some from other books, some of my own, sometimes. There's another on this dirty page, on madness, and the "scarlet speck" that floats in our brains, triggering insanity.

Oscar Wilde knew. He must have. I've seen that speck. I've seen lots of specks. Can see wisps of blueness drift from square lights on the roof like gas. Carpet looks deeper too.

4

Ian thinks two jobs are too much for me. He smirks and says 'you're a psycho' when he cleans out rats' cages. That's usually when he talks about my jobs, before I leave for the library in the mornings. But here I am, outside Curby Health Promotion, no afternoon breakdown. Not yet.

But smoking at the door? There's too much air here, too much nature. Smoke pollutes nettle smells. Makes you feel guilty. Poor, innocent nettles. I need guilt though. Want to suffer.

Frank's waiting for me inside. I smoke outside. Have to. Want to be disgusted. No, want to feel guilty for being disgusted at Fairfields, this endless scheme of concrete horizons, cold blocks, dazed populace, dark haze. Guilt helps you work here.

Frank took me for a tour in his new car, a customised 'Ford Consul GT', used in 'The Sweeney' he said, on my first day at Curby Health Promotions. We passed tenements with windows slashed with vertical blinds, usually cream, and Frank said that, inside every house, were 'possibilities for collective action'. We had to provide the glue, he said, and his eyes were smiling in a religious way. Frank's all skin; his brown hair's hidden by its flatness, so his eyes compensate, I think.

We passed the post office and Jan's chemist's. Two young women in tracksuits were fighting and Frank had to slow to steer around their dogs and tiny children, who were wandering on the road. I saw Jan's face at the chemist's window and tried to wave but Frank sped up and said that Maslow's 'Hierarchy of Needs' was based on a middle-class perception of the lower classes being 'Neanderthal'. When we returned to Curby

Health Promotions, the afternoon sun had painted an oily rainbow on its window.

Look at Fairfields Community Lounge entrance now, with its tinted window from the 80s cracked in the corner, with hardened egg stains. Look at its dinted CCTV cameras, barbed wire on the roof like the piss-stained grocer and off-license next door.

This place creeps around you like jagged things in the dark. Am I in a documentary? No…an urban horror?

Where's the sky? Look up, no sky. Who could live here, really? There're too many multi-storeys, tenements, too much tension. Who built this shit? Cold shadows scraping me.

Listen. The cleaner is singing inside. A country and western tragedy. I'll walk in; she'll stop singing, skulk at me, hobble a bit while her white hair twitches. Her eyes are more credible than mine. She doesn't trust me. Want to know her but fucking hate her.

My phone's vibrating. It'll be Frank wanting to know if I'm okay, where I am. Right, go in, slide along the wet floor, past the cleaner.

Frank's whispering to Pete beside the boiling kettle. Pete volunteers here, doing admin. He's *looking for direction* after his wife left with the kids. Wish he'd start wearing deodorant. Maybe iron something. Wash his hair, shave. Stop breathing like that.

Look at this office. Brown light leaks from table lamps with yellowed shades. Frank brought them in to make the place seem informal. There's no window but there're window plans, waiting for funding, always. There're folders crammed into dullness. Can hardly see my table in the corner but see my pc. Pete's answering the phone at his table beside the sink. He always coughs before he says anything.

Think there're shadows in the bloodstream now. I've been infected! Stop...good, now work, research; *have* to raise awareness of the poor health of the underprivileged of Curby. Like a good middle class man. Or am I middle class? Frank likes my writing though. It's simple, informative, he usually says, when his eyes are too genuine for me, too human, too 'person-centred'.

'Kettle's just boiled Paul. Cuppa mate?'
    'Tea please Frank.'
    'You okay today, you look fuckin' knackered.'
    'I'm fine Frank.'

He doesn't smile but there's one hiding under his flat lips, you could tell by his eyes again, the way they glisten reassuringly and his naked face is still.

'So how's the research coming along Paul?'
    'I'm sourcing really relevant data.'
    'Sourcing relevant data? Brilliant, sounds fuckin' marvellous. Here's your tea mate, get it fuckin' down ya.'

Frank leaves me at my desk. He trusts me to write reports but I jot down extras for short stories, poems, scripts. Haven't written one yet but it's coming...soon.

Pete's going to cough, his face's preparing. There it goes, loud and dry like wood being broken in a pigeon shed. Now he's going to speak to someone. Hope it's not...no, it's not me; he's looking at Frank at his desk behind me.

'Frank, what was your idea again, about raising awareness?'

'Oh yeah. Well Pete, I'd like to raise awareness of the link between poverty and poor health, start a wider research campaign, get media support, gather plenty of evidence, lobby an MEP for welfare reform, free school meals, more clinics in disadvantaged areas, that sort of shit. Link it all together.'

'Y'see, that's a fuckin' *great* idea Frank! Let's do it! Why don't we do it now?'

Christ, I've not typed a word into Google and Pete's getting emotional. I don't want to look at him. So don't. But his stoop's so drawing. Oh, but there's a gleam on his face. Usually he speaks then shrivels. No, he looks sharper.

It's hate. He hates me. His eyes are shuddering because he's trying not to look at me. Nope, he's staring now, his face's fighting a grin. Another cough's imminent. And there it goes. Oh god…something doesn't feel right.

'Frank, why are we not *all* fighting for this? Let's do it! Why isn't Paul doing something? Fucksake!'

'Paul's busy researching. He'll get involved when we've had time to plan things mate, okay?'

And he retreats into a flump. He'll not talk to Frank unless he's passing on phone messages. He *never* talks to me.

I don't want him to talk to me. Don't want to be here. I do this to punish myself. Doctor says so. But I *need* to be here: it's the perfect gloom. This whole office's shaded, like a giant's leering over us, watching. Look at Pete's dark face. He could be glowering, I wouldn't know. Frank's whispering behind me.

Hoover's humming next door. Phone's ringing. Thank fuck, the phone's ringing! Paul coughs.

'Good morning, Curby Health Promotion? Yeah, he's here, can I ask who's calling…right. Frank! It's Suzie!
    'Right Pete. Ask her to call back later. I've got a meeting soon.'
    'Suzie, Frank says can you call him back lat…hey, there's no need for that, Frank's a busy man! Well fuck you too, you…!'
    'Pete, just put the phone down!'
    'Sorry Frank, but she pissed me…'
    'It's alright.'

I'm sure another woman phoned for Frank yesterday. Wasn't her name Liz? Did I answer the phone? Or did it happen at all?

Feels like night now. Computer keys click as my hand shakes like it's been dismembered. They don't care, don't see it, don't sense anything, sitting in their hardness of numbers, aims, poverty. So make another cuppa.
    Fuck! If I walk to the kettle I'll have to pass through these lumps of darkness around the office. Look at them, like iron clouds. Can hear them creak, uh! Well don't listen. Stay still. Don't look at anything. You'll be out in three hours. Okay, look down at the table then, you're allowed that. Look at the grooves in the wood. Sparks playing in there, acute psychotic episode, tickling my head, isn't it, my lack of insight, no social acceptance, they'll never get it, stop, quickly, methodical, no, not good, need coffee, but it's a trigger, fuck it, here goes!

Afternoons are getting harder then. I could have cried

in there. But I'm out now and look, this bus stop's new. Used to be fields here though. Probably dead vegetables, under this concrete. Mum brought me here. Or was it here? To take photographs of a standing stone. An old flash camera. It was raining, it was midnight. She was wearing a green Mackintosh with a hood, couldn't see her face. I didn't have a coat, lost a shoe, heard her laugh, then cry. The stone's gone now. No one talks about it. Maybe it didn't exist. Should I exist? Stop it, here comes the bus, get home.

5

This flat is rented. Not many rented flats in Riverview. You sense desperation here: mortgages give relief. Soon they'll have mortgage plasma on intravenous drips in hospitals, emergency equity clinics.

Everything's new here: flats, villas, shops, gym on land where a linoleum factory once stood, outside the city centre. I was lucky to get this place. Put down 'Bipolar One' on the application form, got a call from a woman called Denise with a sexy lisp who said I was repositioned on the waiting list because I met 'thertain criteria'.

Smell that? It's newness: on cream walls in the lounge, pine in the bathroom, tiles on the kitchen wall, metal rims on spotlights on the roof in the hall. Fresh enough to obsess over. I've never lived like this before.

Have I ever lived before? Should I die? Now that's a medical question. Yes, of course it is, I suffer from 'a suspension of existence', did you read over the handout, a common sign of depression Mr Belardo, record this thought, analyse it if you wish, but accept it. Yeah, well, feels typical enough. Stop it, make tea, I can survive anything. I've survived today so fuck off doctor.

There, see, you *can* let it pass. Look at your face in the mirror; acknowledge yourself as a mood warrior, or something less archaic maybe.

I had to move this mirror up the wall when I moved in. It only reflected my throat.

My face's complicated though. I despise it like everyone else. Look at my left eye, mostly covered with discoloured lid, looks like penis skin next to my other eye. One cheek bone's higher than the other. My nose looks broken, thick mouth sags at the left corner where saliva gathers in frothy pools. I'm monstrous.

Jan likes my face though. Says it's interesting. She'd like to do a cast of it, put it on a wall after she leaves her husband. She could place it above a fireplace.

My walls are empty. No framed photographs. They're dangerous. I burnt them. Doctor called them 'triggers'. Especially ones with Wendy and Kate...now don't start, stop right there. Okay, good.

Jan's never been here. No woman's ever been here. Probably wouldn't feel right anyway.

Invited Christine here after the library Christmas social last year because she'd never seen *Bram Stoker's Dracula*. She got in a taxi with me. When we got here she changed her mind. Said my face was red and I looked tired. I broke a toe when I got in the house because I kicked the wall. I was aiming for air.

My face's red now. There's black in the mirror too. If I don't blink it covers the glass. Stop looking...fuck off.

No, I have to do something. Oh, yeah, the recordings. Doctor gave me sheets. There they are. Sit down, write, that's the phone ringing, ignore it, write, come on...

Right, the physical stuff, in this column, where, there, under *what were you feeling*, quick! Well today I had shaking in the morning, doctor, in legs and arms, and some numbness at lunchtime in my soul. Oh, and weakness, hand trembles, I nearly forgot. And of course nausea at the bus stop, but that always happens; waiting makes me want to vomit but what about the sparkles in my eyes though? No, leave it out. He'll want to change things again.

Oh god, the thoughts column. Record them, here, under *what were you thinking*, hurry, or is it *what are your rational* thoughts? Stop it, must be methodical, mood diaries...reduce episode duration, yes, do it quickly then, come on. Oh that fuckin' phone! So, feeling disconnected in the afternoon because I detest...no, too subjective...feeling like something's being sucked out my heart as I write this...again, too vague, he doesn't like that. Well fuck you doctor...no, must examine negative thought process...no, leave it, the phone...god! Okay, in the morning, felt like I was being threatened by myself...no, too open to analysis. Words are useless. What's out the window, *don't* answer the phone!

Outside, Compton Bridge, so look at it, now, and the River Bow, yes, above light pollution from flat windows and wasn't the bridge named after a councillor who died of bowel cancer? Yes it was. He ran in a marathon over the bridge when it was opened to 'raise awareness' of the disease, remember? Yes, he died and why am I not dead yet? I can answer that phone, but why should I, and the fat shit collapsed on the finish line, Councillor Compton, like he ran to death for the public, but at least he escaped phones and Ian can't see anything apart from garage walls from the council semi he shares with Mandy and Karl in Fairfields, can he? He can't see yellow lights on the bridge flicker, fuckin' phone, or the darkness but the river's too urban for reflection and why can't I answer the fucking phone, the phone, the *phone*!

Phone won't stop ringing! I'm coughing! I want to die! Rip out my own...

'Hello?'

'Hi Paul it's Jan. Listen, I was thinking…I want us to make a porn film.'

'Okay.'

'Nothing too graphic. Maybe filmed through a window, you know, into a room. Like we've been caught on CCTV. I'll book us a room in a hotel in the city centre'

'Yeah.'

'And I'd like photographs of us. Maybe of us doing it in my car. We can position a camera somewhere. I've got a digital camera and Penny will print them off for me, you know, her in the maintenance place.'

'Oh yeah, Penny from the computer maintenance place.'

'So, when then?'

'Whenever you like.'

'I'll arrange it.'

'Yeah.'

'How're the new meds?'

'Interesting.'

'Okay, night night.'

'Bye Jan.'

Hate putting the phone down, hate it, *hate* it! Expect an echo. But I'm always disappointed. It would grow louder as a camera panned out to show this room with one futon, coffee table with white laptop on it, music system in the corner (bought at a police auction - only five pounds but I really wanted the stuffed dog) and me, standing by the door, looking insane beside my green Victorian chair that no one ever sits in because no one's ever here.

Phone rattles when I touch it, look. Futon's frame cracking as I sit. Legs protest at me, straight out, the cramps. So uniform, aren't they, an organised pain, absolutely equal, down both sides. A union ache!

Wish my throat was being slit, right now, I mean it, again and again and again by someone who knows I'm the most evil fucker on earth, the blood a fountain of relief, the blade sharp enough for quickness...I'd like to be murdered quickly. Couldn't bear prison. Solitary confinement, though...yeah, that'd be alright.

Hate sobbing like this. So pathetic. Sound like a soap actor.

The meds...take the last pill. Go to bed.

6

Okay. Make tea then. You always do. That will start it though. Good. Now see who I am. Look out the window or something. 5:30 am. A dark June morning like the others this week and I am...Paul Belardo. Watch suited neighbours slip into silver and black cars, speaking into mouthpieces.

Listen to the news on the radio. What *is* the best British breakfast? Phone in with suggestions, win something. Six Iraqis dead. Another drought in Africa. Credit crisis. Floods down south. So he's a Weetabix man? I would have thought he'd be a porridge type.

Arm feels like someone else's. Even looks alien, too long. Okay. More tears to come then. Oh, and suicidal thoughts, lovely...quiet, soft, painless like the song, constant image of blood dripping from my wrists, noiseless, into a black vacuum. Cosy though, isn't it? Back to bed later then, obviously, could be for a week, could be two. Maybe an hour away.

Shower. Let it come. Maybe the meds will perform.

That's better. Get dressed. Take a pill. Phone in sick. Say it's leprosy or something, who fucking cares.
  Go for the old black jeans and t-shirt. They've been there on the floor since January, when I wrote 'in bed with black jeans and t-shirt, day three, can't move, can't see past arms around my head, but these clothes are good to wear in bed'. Mood diaries, cognitive behavioural therapy, curb episodic duration. Now into the lounge, let it come, listen to the radio: someone's phoned in, won a digital personal organiser,

congratulations John from Suffolk.

Floor is fluid. Oh, watch it! Sit down then. Radio's playing 'Wichita Lineman' by Glen Campbell, a soothing country and western-easy listening hybrid that effectively portrays the paradox of the human condition of wanting to be loved but desiring loneliness. A car alarm's gone off outside; an electric voice murmurs a warning. It's related to me, must be. Come on, stop it! But they'll know it was me! But I haven't done anything though, surely! Have I? But there's got to be some connection, why else would it…

Phone's ringing. Oh god why do I have a phone…where is it? I have to move, I can't move. No, leave it. Shit. I'm coming, I'm over there.

'Uh, hello?'
  'Paul?'
  'Yeah…yeah?'
  'It's Jan. I _ it's early'
  'Hi.'
  'Listen, _ calls last night.'
  'Right. What? What…I'm feeling…'
  '_ film, remember?'
  'No. I'm feeling…'
  'So _ video camera_ night.'
  'Night? I'm not understanding…'
  ' _ usual place at 6 _ ? _ later in the city centre.   .'
  'I…don't know if…'
  'Great. See _ . You okay?'
  'No…not really…something's wrong.'
  'Speak to _ . _ ready for work. Bye.'
  'Uh…right…'
Get back on…the futon. God, can hardly move though. Feel…like an….astronaut, the Urban Spaceman, The

Bonzo Dog Dooda Band, a perfect fusion of psychedelic fun and eccentric Englishness and *wow*, look at that! Everything's curving...towards centre...coffee table's warping... music centre...CDs versus vinyl...and my old friend Eric sold all his albums and we got pissed with the money, it was Valentine's Day...my varnished floorboards are melting. Like a picture on a broken TV...watched Wimbledon on acid once with Eric and he cried when a ballboy fell...Well...*this* is new though.

What's this? Something's drilling...into my skull! Fuck! Or maybe...it's a migraine...Mother's excuse...in bed.

Jesus, stomach's blackmailing me.

Now I'm not cleaning that. Leave it. I deserve to live like this...scum, I'm fucking scum.

Oh, everything's black and white now...crowded with...strange grains in the air. Car alarm outside sounds recorded, played back. Vomit pool's lost its pungency or can you smell your own? Legs stinging, cold...yeah, I've pissed myself. Okay. This is major.
    Oh ho, right, okay then, fair enough. Lie back, let it spread, it's alright. It's the meds, that's all, probably. You *know* that...so close your eyes, let it work then, what's the problem? For fucksake, you always do this, you cowardly cunt!
    Whoa! No, bad idea, sit up. Come on, sit up! That's it. Sit here for...a while. It's spreading, so leave it then, but what'll happen?

Maybe you should move around, but what'll happen? Jesus! Feel like...don't know...I've just left myself behind, forgotten me! Right, phone doctor, okay. Right now! Emergency appointment! Tell them! Probably need an ambulance. No, not hospital, *never* hospital, not with the dream people in the smoking shelter…Or should I leave it? Interesting. Yeah, let it all come on, stop being such an arsehole!

Phone's ringing *again!* Get up, answer it. Get up! Crawl to the phone you fucking evil, worthless…bastard.

'Huh…who…w…'
    'Paul, it's Ian. Sorry for _ early.'
    'Hi…phone…the doctor…'
    'The _ freaking you out?'
    'Uh…yeah…phone…'
    'Well _ suffer mate.'
    'Uh hu…but…'
    'I'm suffering _ Paul.'
    'Got…to…'
    'Mandy's _ me out.'
    'Uh…wha…'
    'I _ , unbelievable. She said _ too intense. _ believe that?'
    'Wh…'
    '*I'm having _ on Karl.* Honestly, _ said! _ told me to fuck off. What a _ !'
    'Hngh…aah…'
    'What? Anyway _ for a pint _ ? _ pissed. We can _ Victorian pub you   still got _ . Brighton's _ !'
    '…uum…'
    ' _ get yourself off these _ . _ the shop later.'

Get to the bathroom. Throw face in sink. Cold water. Hurry! Ugh! Move your legs! Come on! That's it! Up we go. That's it! Towards the door.

This way! Come on! Oh no what's this? Blackness? No! Can't see anything, oh god help me, save me, damn me, you wanker, can't see…anything…cunt…falling…into…nothing…there's nothing…there…stupid…bastard…fuck...mother…Wendy…Kate.

7

Wait. How did I get up here? Where was I before? I'd collapsed. Oh no...but how *can* I be here? There's no space for me, it's not possible but I'm here now, between the top of the door and the ceiling. I can see the lounge, out the window, look, but how *can* I be here? Right, you probably got on mobile stairs, tried to hang yourself, with...like that time in the caravan, but there's no part of me to see, so...where's my FUCKING BODY! Oh god, how can I be here looking without eyes, without a body, without...oh good god.

Calm down. It's a hallucination. Phew, yeah, you've had them before, wrong prescription, 1998, arrested in a market in Kavos, seeing dogs' faces on people, shaking in the square but it wore off, this should wear off, it's the meds, they've gone wrong, Doctor said, 12%, so it'll *end*, won't it, come on!

But...how can I *think*, can't see me, nowhere, Jesus Christ, but I'm here, thinking! Can hear me, doctor said I had to hear myself when I was up, but not like this and I've *never* asked anyone for anything, haven't done anything, why would anyone want this to happen to me? Oh you *cunt*, what have I done?

Stop. I can't!

Why do I...nothing but feeling, no breathing, this corner's soft, so how can...oh no, stop! That's it. Good. Come on! Take some time, that's it now.

Familiar though. Felt this before. I *know* it happened, this feeling, walking home with dad, our third home, he was quiet. We stopped outside. Yes, that's what happened, saw mum up at the blue window, television on behind her, no lights. Still, staring, no real face, hiding her hands, that was it, yeah, felt myself lift away from dad's side. He didn't talk, but I knew I was floating. How did I do that then? I've done it again.

Okay. This is it. I've done it. Could be dead. Everything's over. I'll burn soon. I'm a sinner, they've been waiting. Come on then! Nobody there? What, this is my hell? Is this it? '98 was worse. I saw dogs' faces, ripped off my own face.

Not that bad though, is it. Lounge's not changed, but should it have changed? It's still black and white, but more tubular, yeah, like I'm watching a programme about my lounge on a black and white television, from up here, isn't it? Or like watching grainy horrors in bed with mum, except there're no cuddles and crying, or dad next door. Sound's still pre-recorded here, that's not changed, and the radio's still on, voices hissing about lifestyles, diets, re-mortgaging.

I've overdosed, I must have, but I've only taken four. Right, can't be dead, so it's a dream, an out-of-body experience. Of course!

Jan had one once. Her husband screwing her, she watched from the bedroom roof, her death face looking up at her from under that hairy back on their white bed. I've never seen his face, don't know his name, don't fucking care.

So that's what this is, al*right*, could stay like this, what's the problem here, it's better than death.

Everyone's gone. Only me and Ian now.

But what are these things? Dots circling in currents round the room. Dust, but grey, with pins of light inside each grain and…they…make up everything, they *are* everything. Flowing into table form, futon, music centre, walls, window, but why haven't I noticed before? But I *have*.

Watched them play in bus window rain, when I've stared at a bulb until I slept, seen them rage in the dark, so everything's made up of these grains, moving in, moving out of us! Snowstorms of existence! Yeah, I like that, always knew anyway. We could disperse, couldn't we, and blow.

Think I like this, can't move from here anyway, nothing to move. Okay then, I'm legitimate, pass a DLA form. I've done it, how can I be made to do anything and I've got radio, the window over there, Compton Bridge, the river, can see it, don't need anything, can't kill myself now, even if...I might blink out though. Easy.

Look, over there, there're shadows moving, through the grains, hard to tell if they're...they look human. Oh. Ignore them.

What's that noise? Someone's in the shower! Jesus, I've been murdered! Who was it? Oh god!

So am I dead then...*fine*. Fantasy realised, isn't it, but where will they bury me, not with mum and dad in the crematorium, oh god, the wall with the metal doors rusted with rain, and it's always raining there, why does it have to rain? But where's my body? And who would kill me though? What did I do? Do people kill each other anymore? For what? I haven't done anything, have I?

Jan, and Christine, they need me, what will they do? I can't be there, was I ever there, they'll cry though, won't they? I hope they cry, Ian will, he'll be there, at my funeral, won't you cousin? And you can bring

Mandy and Karl, it doesn't matter cousin. Maybe they'll bury me beside my caravan.

Can't see blood anywhere though, no body, murderer must be clean then, efficient. Could be my old friend Eric; he has OCD but what did I do to him? I must have done something, poor Eric, now you're a murderer and you'll kill yourself in your cell in two years, won't you? No more progressive rock albums, you loved them and I made you sell them for beer, now it's only your glasses and your rituals and your stoned-washed denim coat and you must have stabbed me. How could you stab me like that, I loved you, I think.

It must be him, in the shower, cleaning my blood of his arms twenty times, scrubbing his clothes twenty three times, wiping fingerprints off everything, can't wait to see him polish that coffee table, fumigate the air of murder smells.

The shower's stopped. Someone's thumping, down the hall, coming in here...no, into the bedroom. Who is it? Must be Eric; he's a heavy man isn't he and he's moving things, in my wardrobe, taking clothes, bank card, everything. Great, hated it, take it, I've never been real and here he is, here comes my murderer, opening the door, right now! Walking through, underneath me!

Oh no, oh no, oh god *no*. Look! How can it...it's...me? Uh...oh wha...walking round the room...what am I...spraying bleach onto the vomit pool, piss on the futon, walking through these charcoal atoms...they're swirling around me, dancing, surging in and out and I'm picking up fags, from the table, putting them in that brown leather coat I haven't worn all year, that white t-shirt, blue cords. Ah, I'm turning around...Oh Jesus Christ! I don't *know* I'm up here; I'm standing beneath me, looking down the hall!

Oh what *is* this? This is…well, this is *serious* psychosis; obviously, doctor said there'd be…I need a doctor *now*, but he…but *I* don't know I'm here, so how…

Oh my face! I'm smiling; it's not my smile. I wouldn't. Normal eye's fogged, mouth's lost its droop, not enough saliva. Look human but...automatic and now I'm leaving, whistling…country and western! The door's slammed!

Where have I gone? To work? Like that? They'll notice! Christine will see something's wrong, Frank will…no, he wouldn't though. He's too dedicated to notice anything.

I felt nothing when they left. All of them. Nothing.

How long before I blink out then, will I blink out? I need to get a message to someone. This is psychosis, so it's curable. And someone will notice I'm…that *he's* sick. Once they see that face out there, they'll advise it to get help, get new meds. Jan'll notice and I've got, or *he's* got an appointment soon anyway.

Nothing to do but wait Paul. Nothing else you can do. Watch the specks or something. They're animated, rushing, sparking when they merge. Shadows are stronger now too; children of blackness, playing. Radio presenter's talking about wellbeing and stigma and he's playing 'What the World Needs Now is Love' by Jackie DeShannon.

I'm a murderer, a sinner. I can die, I can live…I can wait.

8

Phew! Right! Yes, feel it in my spine, legs. Pure electricity, divine energy! The surge of the universe, inside me! Oh yes, like last summer, *god*, in June, the mood diary recorded a 'day of divine energy and utter peace'. Doctor hummed when he read it. But I wrote something better that day, a poem, but threw it in the fire. Didn't Robert Louis Stevenson burn the first draft of...so why is this problematic then? But the doctor would recognise signs, wouldn't he? Alter medications. A pharmaceutical thought cap.

But thought changes things. The library, I can change that...oh, look, there's Ian with a lizard, smell of piss and chocolate...it's the library system. It's dysfunctional, that's it! Students should access blurbs on the *content* of texts when they highlight database titles. With key paragraphs, chapter headings. They could skim sources without borrowing books, standing in queues, getting lost in irrelevance. Referencing materials would be available, without trawling aisles. Yeah! A title's not enough! I'll tell Christine.

What do students really want anyway? Originality on wet afternoons. Not hours searching. God, I feel fucking great!

We should...look, he's got a baby iguana...offer rooms for guest speakers famous in all disciplines to...it's trying to bite him...facilitate discussions on themes relevant to students *and* the wider world!

'Put the kettle on Paul! Quick! This iguana's freaking out!'

'Right Ian.'

And there's Frank, he could make connections with the

library, why not? He could organise seminars on the realities of community development. On how 'selective intervention', his mantra, can aid the establishment of social justice. He can invite related workers, an interagency effort, to offer their...where's the kettle...there it is...he's got ginger nuts today...reflections on the voluntary sector. Have to write this down. Ian'll have paper somewhere.

'Ian, got any paper?'

'Beside the till. Hurry up and give me a hand with these turtles. That bastard iguana just bit me!'

'Right Ian.'

Christine will listen to me. Frank's receptive to ideas, if they're absorbable into his mission. This'll open the library to the rest of Curby. Social change is possible. Students will benefit from increased...kettle's clicked...blue spark on the handle...has something else just been switched on...there's some paper...intellectualisation. Meetings can be advertised in the Curby Gazette. Everyone interacting above the class morass! Why has no one thought of this? It's so simple! Library's the key! Wish I could see Christine's tits. Just once.

Kate didn't have nice tits. Too mottled. Saw them in Curby Leisure Centre the first time. An accident, she was swimming. They flopped out when she climbed from the water. The pool attendant rushed over with a towel and slipped. Cracked his elbow on the tiles. I laughed. Kate cried. She cried a lot. We should never have met.

'Christ, what took you? Cheers Paul. Tea, how can we live without it eh?'

'Yeah, it'd be impossible. We've a long history of...'

'So we still okay for tonight? What's that Victorian pub called again?'

Libraries are distant, Frank says. Officious, unwelcoming. But he's not spent holidays in them as a child. Easters and summers in Curby Central Library. Sci-fi and crisps. Gothic horror and plastic blinds bleached by magnified sunshine. Reading until tea-time, oh god yes, bitter air-freshener making my head ache, beautiful pain!

Frank knows nothing. He'll retire, tell stories of his fight against social injustice in forgotten bars in nothing-days to no one. He'll have no one. Suzie will leave him and...wonder what she looks like? And who is Liz? Oh...what...

'Tonight?'

'I phoned you this morning, you spacer! Mandy's chucked me, hasn't she? I need to get pissed, desperately.'

'Oh.'

'You were all over the place on the phone. So meet me at nine, at the...god, what's it called?'

'The Satanic Mill, in Court Square?'

'That's the one! Bring money with you this time.'

Libraries are filled with possibility. Frank could never understand. Why am I not there now? Walking along the aisles, passing endless connections to anything, to more than this...Oh god, can feel it, there it is, rushing over my head, like light, the energy of the universe! I'm part of it. Oh fuck the diaries, learn to recognise your own symptoms, yes doctor, euphoric mood, present in mania, but how could this be wrong? Yes, oh yes, feel it surge, but stop the tears coming though, Ian will notice. Legs are trembling, oh my god…I'm going to change everything…oh yeah, there's Ian…

'Okay. So where will you live?'
    'I'll crash at yours tonight. Do you know…do you know what Mandy said?'

The library can show films. Innovative, related to disciplines, but accessible, a mirror for Curby, to show them who they are and who they're not. Didn't James Joyce, yes he did, with *The Dubliners*, made them all look, didn't he! I'll change them, but the films haven't been made yet. Need art contacts, Christine will know…and…

'Mandy said I'm ignorant, self contained. You believe that?'
    'Self contained?'
    'Yeah I know! She said I was closed off, didn't understand the world, understand her and Karl's *needs*. I hate that word! *Needs*. Mandy's changed since she started college.'

Right, okay then. Need to see Christine. Arrange a meeting between her and Frank. This will take a lot of preparatory work. Get ideas listed then. Yes, first, conceptualise it. Write it up. Show Frank. Convince him. Make the benefits glimmer on the page. Yes! Source possible funding. Why hasn't anyone else thought of…Create questionnaires? See Christine's tits. Kill yourself. Join the universe. Wendy. No.

'Mandy needs an outlet, needs to be *going somewhere*, wants to do an Open University course next year, but feels that *moving right now would disrupt Karl's education*. I'm a selfish bastard who should be thinking of their goals. But I'm forty - five Paul!'

'I know.'

'If I don't make a move now I'll never make it! She doesn't get it!'

'So what're you going to do?'

'Go to Brighton, do some market research, price accommodation, source suppliers.'

'When?'

'I don't know. You look different Paul. Not been sleeping again? Have you been to that tanning place?'

'Ha, no. Anyway, what's the point? I could never match your natural brown. So why not go to Brighton next week then, close the shop?'

Oh look, it's one of Ian's smiles. This one means he's thinking. Or delaying thought to linger in nothing. Hurry up! God, need to get to the library. Nothingness is a killer. Ian, you succumbed years ago. New TVs, leather settee, family, soap operas. Poison. I have to escape.

'I can't just leave Paul. It's not that simple.'

'Yeah right. Okay Ian, I'll see you tonight then. I've got an early start at the library.'

'Right then Paul. And get off them meds; you look like you're speeding.'

'Okay Ian.'

'And Paul.'

'Yeah?'

'Watch yourself mate; you've got a hard-on poking up your cords.'

'Oh.'

When will this place open? They're late. Come on! Can't wait outside here with these students with scarves and Oxfam expressions. They smell of nothing. They *mean* nothing. Petted children. Pride of parents who debate in dining rooms, eat organic vegetables, discuss 'issues' on the PTA. Where are their real faces? Every action's diluted. And they're all in bronze air. Interesting. Some atmospheric interference, Pink Floyd, Eric and his band…stop.

Hey, fuck me too. I belong here, I'm one of them. Once a child with expectations. A boy with educated children for parents.

There's Christine coming to open up with old John, the security guard. Oh thank the lord!

'Good morning Christine! What a glorious morning! Listen, I've been thinking…'

'Good morning Paul. I'm afraid things are a tad unorganised this morning, we've had an incident.'

'Yeah, so I've got some important ideas I'd like to...'

'I'll hear them later if you don't mind.'

'Christine I…'

'Just carry on as normal Paul.'

'Why, what's…?'

'Someone threw bricks through the second floor windows last night, around the back. They were wrapped in newspaper and faeces. A smoke bomb was thrown too. It fizzled out quickly but there's damage in the reference section. I have to divert the students away until the police finish their inquiries. There's graffiti on the side doors. I'll catch up with you later.'

'What's the graffiti like?'

'It's…someone sprayed the words…that…'

'Yes? You can tell me Christine.'

'Someone's sprayed *fuck books.*'

'Oh my god.'

Look, Christine's boobs, they look even better in a

crisis; that glow around her, very amber.

9

Why does everyone in Fairfields argue as if an audience's viewing them? There're open windows *everywhere*. Maybe invisible cameras float outside, filming families in white tracksuits.

Maybe they act for an imagined judge hovering in the home, for endorsements of their existence. They'll be graded for incapacity, life-long sick notes for the winners. Or a permanent crisis loan.

Listen, a man's shouting because his son's stolen from him again to 'keep that little slut' supplied in Dihydracodeine. Someone's smashed a window, thrown used nappies into a communal garden where 'Urban Volunteers' gathered used needles last week. Someone screams at her daughter, who's just called her a 'junkie fuck', threatening her with a hired beating from a girl her own age. An older woman begs a man to go to the chemist's before she stabs herself with a potato peeler. Ha, Jan will serve him.

This Community Lounge should've been built near countryside, so I could smoke in peace.

Right, tell Frank about that plan then. It's the only way to link the university to schemes like Fairfields, to the disadvantaged. Hate that word though, *disadvantaged*. As if the middle classes built a moat around here, screened it off with television walls, drained...oh, who's this...wow.

'Is Frank in there?'
    'Probably, I've not been in yet.'
    'Are you Paul?'
    'Yeah, Paul Belardo.'

'Right, thought so. Listen, has Frank been leaving the office a lot over the last month?'

'Couldn't say really. So you must be Liz…Suzie?'

'Yeah, I must be. So you won't tell me?'

'Honestly, I can't recall.'

'Frank's a bastard.'

'Really?'

'Tell everyone. Were you with him last night?'

'No, can't remember, or I don't think…'

'He didn't come home last night. Didn't phone. Fucker!'

'Oh. I'm sorry to…'

'Don't be!'

Look at her! Long hair so black it's blue. Naked arms like treated wood. Face of a beautiful rodent. Never seen a woman in a black leather waistcoat. Look, she's topless underneath. Sweat oil sliding over skin, rage crimson, towards perfect…she's staring at me. Shit! I'm scared! Cool.

She smells of marijuana and sweat. Haven't smelt weed since I slit my wrists in the girls' toilet at Curby Heights High when I was twelve. A girl was smoking a joint in the next cubicle. We talked about UFOs and her pregnancy before I passed out. Say something before she leaves then, quickly, you arsehole!

'Sorry, Frank's probably in the office.'

'You've already said.'

'Right.'

She's running into the lounge, denim legs strong, buckling her over her Dr Martins. Need her number. Never needed anything so much, *never*. She'll murder me or fuck me. Both sound good. Frank's too committed to social justice for sex anyway. Once I link

Curby Health Promotion with the library, he'll have no space in his head for...she's coming out again, red eyes from the dark. She's walking past, trailing turbulence, and black spots, pulsing. *Wow*. Loving this!

'Suzie...is that your...Suzie!'
   'What?!'
   'Can I...sorry, can I have your number?'
   'Why would I give my number to *you*?'
   'I saw your flyer once, in the office. Something about gardening?'
   'Oh did you?'

She's going to hit me. Quick, look unsure.

'Well, maybe not gardening then. Sure it was something to do with gardens.'
   'And?'
   'Well, I've got a patch of a communal back garden, down at Riverview.'
   'Never heard of it.'
   'It's down by the river, not far from the city centre.'
   'And why are you telling me this?'
   'It needs some work. Thought maybe you'd...'
   'Right.'

I lied. There're car parks, pavements. Look, her face's changing. Looks less animalistic. Some thought has stalled her into a human.

'Take this.'
   'Oh...thanks.'

It's a card, fawn with embossed black italics: S. Hall, Freelance Garden Design, 07590890669. Cool.

Frank's splashing water onto his face at the sink. Pete's gnawing air at his table. Cleaner barges past me to collect the paper waste bin. They're all cartoons.

Frank's turning around. His face isn't so flat anymore: cheek looks red, swollen. He's padding it with a damp cloth. Office gloom's more intense. Don't mind. Can see some fuzz of light.

'Alright Paul, how're things mate?'
'Okay Frank. What happened to your face?'
'Nothing mate, nothing at all. Get yourself a cuppa; I've got some research ideas to put past you.'

Pete growls, shuffles, grins before the phone rings. He coughs.

'I've got some research ideas too Frank. Making links with the university library.'
'Links with the library? What would that achieve?'

Pete smirks like an assassin, writes something on a post-it, passes it to Frank. Frank looks at it, slides it into the back pocket of his blue jeans, his black trainers with white stripes, plain t-shirt.

Sit at my table, switch on pc. Oh, here's Frank, sitting opposite. Oh good god, looks like he's going to preach. His face's stretched, looks betrayed, about to vomit retribution. Want to slash his face with the letter opener on his desk. No, talk him down.

'I think a series of advertised presentations, in the library, on the correlation between disadvantage and poor health and the realities of community work, could raise awareness of this project and its aims while attracting more support out with the voluntary sector, as

well as from people in disadvantaged areas, of course.'
God, did I just say that? I really am shit hot today.
These meds are wonderful!

'Bollocks! Here's a list of questions informed by our last research project. You're going to use them tomorrow to speak to *real* fuckin' people about their health, well being, hopes, fears. It's advertised in the laundrette, butcher's, the pub. Pete went out with posters this morning. Once we've enough data you're going to incorporate it into our current research. We're going to lobby an MEP. Keep focused Paul. Students are passive, useless. It's not Paris in 1968. And here's a newsletter for you to look over. My spelling's shit.'
    'Right.'

I'm going to tear Suzie away from his crusade. Oh god, he's not finished. His eyes are set solid with idealism.

'Listen Paul, people in Fairfields aren't interested in academia. Most people here are switched off from formal education; they see it as part of an oppressive system. It all stems from bad experiences in schools and…'

Wonder if Suzie has to listen to Frank's sermons after sex? Do they ever do it though? He's still talking. He's wrong about everything. I'll still plan the transformation of the library with Christine. Needs someone like me to make links. God it's so simple I feel like I'm going to run out of myself!

He's still talking about schools. I did a shit in the PE block in Curby Heights High before the rest of the class arrived, in the corner of the gym hall on their new plastic flooring. Class was cancelled. So I got pissed with my friend Eric. He started a progressive rock band years later, called 'Maze'. I screwed his depressed girlfriend one New Year's Eve in his bathroom that had a little library of Garfield books. We were all excited because it was the last party with everyone there, before we graduated from university later that summer. Eric and his stonewashed jeans and coat and metallic red glasses, ha…Can't stop my lips from curling. I'm going to laugh! Mobile's hummed. A message from Jan. Oh yeah, Jan!

Rmbr 2nyt c u @ 5 @ arms

See me at 5? What for? God, he's salivating with the thrill of poverty.

'…so the disadvantaged are not going to walk into a university library!'

Good god! Really have to close my eyes, right now, tiredness like a coma! Have to sit in the toilet. Oh look, Frank's leaving too. Good.

10

January by Pilot, a forgotten classic, such an underrated band. Whatever happened to them? Former Bay City Rollers' members David Paton and Billy Lyall were joined by Stuart Tosh and Ian Bairson to form the band in Edinburgh in 1973. "January" was their first hit, followed by "Magic". Now let me take you back to 1977 and the orchestral sounds of ELO....

...so time is a watercolour, painted by a broken artist, flowing while absorbing and I'm being punished, trapped again, still like a smudge in the paint, a mistake in the monochrome, and these little lights, but there are blues when they collide.

Shadows between these pixels aren't moving much: two shapes on the futon, boy sized blackness. Oh what are they, what *is* this?

I'm out there somewhere; *he's* out there, without me. What have I done, who's talked to him? I'll be at Curby Health Promotions by now but Frank won't notice any change in me.

Have to think in bigger ways because this is psychosis, the most severe, *ever*, must be, surely. I'll star in case studies for students to write about on dark afternoons but the meds' effects will weaken soon, won't they?

How to explain this to the doctor when this ends? It will end, it has to, so he'll ask me to read from my mood diary and he'll take notes and I'll say I felt...well, right now, there's a sense...of a loss of my form in a fluid universe, sounds good, can't believe I thought that or I could say it's like being small enough to be invisible, being a kid again, behind a settee. Yeah.

And with that, though, there's comfort in being unseen but…only if you're part of something bigger. Thin comfort though, right now, is it, not a true feeling, but it's alright, isn't so bad. I'll write this down, when I have hands.

Neighbours are getting out of cars outside, listen. Banging doors, talking into mouthpieces about values and wine and it's raining out there, tickling the window, reflections on these pitch grains distorted, scattered, nothing will be the same, will it…oh god.

What was that? The shadows, they're making noises, there's movement. Boyish arm shapes waving. Pixels have stopped flowing, some seeping into the boy shadows, there's colour there, yellow, pink, and other atoms changing the shape of the wall, behind the futon, and the futon itself, all sliding into a scene. New colour, direction, change! This has always been possible, hasn't it, everything's temporary and the radio's playing 'Mr Blue Skies', there's a competition to win a 'Chopper' bicycle and…look, from shadows to boys, standing there, and futon and wall to…

Ha, it's me! *I'm* one of the boys, look at that…when I was nine, maybe ten, Ian's there, the other boy, he'd be twelve, we're in grass behind a shed, and old tyres, rusted bicycle, a burnt tree and there're other council houses, their orange roofs poking above bleached stems. This is Ian's back garden, the home he lived in with his dad, until it burnt down, after Ian left when he was sixteen and the sky's yellow, slits of cartoon pink behind us.

There's someone else, another voice shouting 'okay then' from inside the shed, a girl's and Ian's laughing,

58

oh Ian, what now, and he's talking:

'Come on Paul, it's your turn. She's ready, didn't you hear?'
   'I don't want to.'
   'Still going on about your mum?'
   'She IS coming back!'
   'They won't let her out, I've told you. Ask your dad. You don't care anyway; you're just acting up. You always act up. Look, you doing this or not?'
   'Why…do what?'
   'I've *told* you. Go in and see. Kiss her on each cheek. She'll give you ten pence.'
   'Ten pence?'
   'Yep.'
   'Okay.'
   'Good. Go on then!'
   'I'm going, I'm going.'

Oh no, Fat Anne's naked arse, in a shed with drills, empty lager cans. Oh Jesus, I'm kissing that, she's handing me a coin, she paid me to do that? Oh what did we do to Anne? She's leaving now, her pink jumper with burn stain on the collar, Blondie badge on a sleeve, black ski pants with holes in the knees and Ian's looking at me but he's not smiling. Didn't smile too much then, hadn't learnt that yet, am I dying now? It's alright Paul. Oh, he's talking again. Come on Ian, what are you saying now cousin, it was always me and you:

'See? Feeling better now?'
   'Yeah, suppose.'
   'Girls are hopeless. I mean, look at your mum!'
   'Right, okay then.'
   'So, what's your dad told you about your mum?'
   'She's ill, that's all.'

'Yeah but she's not got the flu, Paul.'
'I know!'

Dots are shifting again like in an Etch-a-Sketch, look, oh but why are they doing this? Do they flow through me, oh it's beautiful, do they get electrified by memory then? That's why they can create like this, it's a natural thing like death and maybe I'm disintegrating. Good. Where's this?

It's…a waiting room. There's me, still ten years old, ha ha, behind an orange plastic chair with a walkie-talkie and there's Ian, look at you Ian, beside a drinks machine with the other one and oh god, there's my dad, Christian Belardo! He's sitting, smoking, wiping his forehead, his spectacles with black frames, shiny and serious, and he's still wearing his lab coat with ballpoints. Look at them, poking from the top pocket, a rainbow of ink and they clicked together when he shivered, that funny noise in my ears sometimes when he lifted me and I swallowed a lid once. He worked at Curby Polytechnic, didn't he; my dad was a chemistry tutor.

But he died, didn't he, Septicaemia they said, tan face black in a coffin and a little Spanish flag, rusty needle pierced his skin but you never talked of the country you left. Why not dad, my Spanish dad, what was wrong with you then? I never visited after I left, I couldn't dad, you must know, but you tried, didn't you.

Wait, look at the guy sitting next to him there, a brown paper bag over his head, there're blood stains on it, on the floor, and an old woman's holding his hand, and a bloody screwdriver but she keeps looking at the clock and sighing. People sighed a lot in places like this, you sighed a lot dad.

Here come two doctors through revolving doors, into the room and there's Ian's dad, my drunken uncle, behind them. Old Philippe taught Spanish in primary schools, but he was good at hiding his drinking. Ian always knew though, you were always smart Ian, I needed you. I need you. He drank in his shed, when Ian was in bed, my uncle Philippe, or when we were out playing at the park, the warped monkey bars and we played until night, didn't we Ian?

A doctor, a Chinese man, talks to my dad and now my dad's following him, asking me to come too and look at me, skipping a bit, he doesn't know, the young me, but I know what's coming, can watch it, this re-run from my head, because that's what this is, isn't it? It's a show from inside, the grains rush through me and sift all of this out of me, they must. But how do they organise themselves like that, into re-creation, into scenes like this? Don't care, or is that true? I hope I don't care because it's like you're stoned now, entertained, watching a film, Children's Film Foundation, but I'm in it and Ian too; look, he's escaped his dad's grasp, running after me, down the longest corridor with paintings of fields on the cream and brown walls. There aren't any humans in the paintings though. No café here, no families here apart from us. It wasn't that type of place, was it?

Oh, right, look, Ian and I, at a large window now that looks into a white ward, funny looking at us like this, as if I'm a camera, floating behind our younger selves, but I like it. There're chairs behind, and a table with a blue ashtray. Remember these big glass ashtrays, looking through them at the sun, the colours. It's there, in a patients' smoking area at the end of the ward, they had ashtrays in hospitals then but there're not many patients. Or maybe they're hiding, apart from a bald man singing, bobbing in a chair. Some yellow mist's

61

floating above the beds. I don't remember that, but it's there, look, I'm watching it in this documentary now, a documentary that's leaked out from my temporal lobe, you'll like that doctor. Dad's asked to walk through a door that the doctor unlocks, into the smoking area and I watch dad sign something. He was always writing, but wrote nothing, only marked essays, didn't he, and the doctor leaves. Dad inspects the ashtray with a red pen and look at me and Ian laughing at him. We were only kids though, weren't we, but he doesn't hear.

The doctor returns, pushing a wheelchair with my mum sitting in it. Mrs Margaret Belardo, it's my mum, oh my god, that human pile, that head lolling like that, foam from her mouth, dripping on her white gown, eyes reeling like an animal that knows it's about to die. And it was stupid, all that Paracetamol, her stomach pumped and she choked...she looks like me but I wanted to look like dad; Spanish, reflective black hair. But mother's genes were strong though, before she slipped into illness, like all of us. We're all slipping, aren't we? But it wasn't his fault though. Nothing ever was, was it? He never did anything, to cause anything, only worry, suffer.

Aw, dad, holding mum's hand, whispering, crying a little into purple fag ash, but she doesn't respond, doesn't recognise him but the young me bangs at the window. Ian laughs and she doesn't see me, she can't turn her head anyway, can't keep her eyes still. Doctor's come back now and she's taken away and dad stirs the contents of the wet ashtray with his pen before he leaves the ward and Ian keeps kicking me. Dad asks me if I'd like to go to Dorset with him next weekend, visit Auntie Jill, and we could take Ian, if Philippe agreed, it would be nice, wouldn't it? There're great beaches but I hate beaches.

Ha, look, I run off, look at me, chasing Ian, shouting into my walkie-talkie, now I'm a policeman but I'm fading away, down the corridor. But wait, isn't this when I…yeah, I've slipped, look at me sliding, along that varnished floor, straight into that man with the bag on his head who's walking with the woman…ha, I knock him over! She screams. He falls down beside me, lies there, he's still, even from up here I can see that one eye through a hole in the bag and it doesn't move, doesn't blink, and that's not a human, that's an animal.

Oh, they're moving again, the dots are changing direction, becoming…room's back. So why did that happen? Okay, take every memory and use them, I don't give a fuck, I'm not a Freudian endnote, I need no explanation, there is no explanation, no so…I'm part of the current though, that's all. It's not personal; they pass through me like rain, that's why they show this. Not good, no, but I'll melt, death by memory film, so I won't watch much then, before I…no, I can't watch that, no Kate or Wendy, can't, please let me go. It's getting dark again.

11

…and there's a link between mania and creativity. Yes, I agree. Doctor was right. Mania does 'produce advantages' in 'creative work'. I feel it. Have always felt it. Wrote eight short stories in two days last summer. But the hospital staff misplaced them. They wouldn't believe that something significant was inside me. I'm part of the swirl of the universe. Attuned now, can use it to do anything. Right now, can't catch the ideas. They're ricocheting. When I catch one, I'll fizzle. With brilliance. No one will believe the results…What's that whirring sound?

'Paul, are you okay? Your eyes are all red *again*.'
    'What…oh, Jan, you're naked…I'm ah…just a bit…'
    'Hurry up and undress.'
    'Oh right. What's that bleeping sound?'
    'It's the camera, you know that. Or it could be the phone; I've taken it off the hook.'
    'Where's the camera?'
    'Over there behind the curtain.'

A hotel room. Of course, the porn film. There's the camera, on the window ledge, behind a net curtain. There's a yellow metallic sticker on it with writing…'P. Dawn's Computer Maintenance and Digital Hire'.
    The room is a clone of Jan's guest bedroom. No pictures, no personality, clinical atmosphere. Only the colour's different. This place's cream. Smells of apples and car upholstery. Not potpourri and detergent.

'Hurry, rub it or something, get it hard. I'm getting

cold.'

'Right, okay.'

Okay then. Think of Christine. Me slurping oats and milk off her tits. Nestling in her red fur. Screwing in the library archive cage with the sensitive tomes. Inhaling the spores of history. Old John catches us, shines his torch as she moans, her face frozen through achieving self- actualisation in a public place and…

'Start with the feet. Ten minutes exactly. Don't make a noise and don't look up at my face.'

'Okay then.'

Oh, what's that noise…someone's shouting outside…something's smashed…

'Did you hear that?'

'Ignore it; it's just hooligans outside.'

'Something smashed.'

'Probably a car window. Come on then!'

'Okay.'

No, we would eat first. In a restaurant, a Spanish one. I'd tell Christine about my plans. She'd unbutton her blouse, two buttons, leave her hand on my arm, listen to me talk about the…Jan should have washed her feet…new databank system with links, public seminars with a focus on universal themes, inclusive, above class strata, yeah. She'd support my ideas, admit her love for me, cry, take my hand, drag me into her Volvo estate…when's she going to move me on from this sole…we'd drive to…the docks, outside Ian's shop, yeah. She'd unzip me and…

'Move up now, be gentle.'

'Right.'

Oh thank god! Right, so, when she's busy doing that I'd keep talking about...an extension onto the library, an extension of *thinking* about its purpose, yeah, a new area with bar and snacks, screening room, chill out zone with futons, bean bags, music, DVDs, games hire...feels different, she must have shaved...yeah, even an adult section, be progressive enough to supply erotica, texts on its cultural significance, expand the intellectual geography of these limp students, bring in the punters...yes, change education!

'Come up here now.'
    'I'm coming.'

Jan's tits. So colourless. Two anaemic mounds. How do they defy gravity? Probably plumped with a drug used by chemists. Her body's loose but confined. And there's an invisible skin of anaesthetic, I can smell it. She gleams with it.
    So, after the Volvo oral it would be up to Riverview where Christine would ask about my family, background, plans while drinking wine...I'd better get some in...no, I won't stop thinking about this, it *is* going to happen, I'm going to *make* it happen...so I'd tell her about my weak Spanish father, eccentric mother, how I'd transform the library, bring education to the disadvantaged...no, the *residents* of Curby, then I'd...what *will* I do...fall off a cliff, what, come on!

'Right, stop, go in me now. Wait till I turn over. What's wrong with you, you look like you're dreaming.'
    'It's the meds. Don't worry about it.'
    'Fine. In you go. And out before you come. Then don't look at me, don't make a noise, dress and go.'

'Of course.'

What will I do…invest, that's it, a new project, new life. Yeah, scout for Ian, in Brighton, for premises. Sell my stationary caravan (I'll never use it again, unless I need to hide), put in collateral, make money. Buy a place in Brighton. Do a masters at a university there, business management. Work in a library to fund it. Ask Christine to move posts to be with me…she'd follow, she will, she'd have to if she wants to be with me…

'Paul! Stop being so hard! My head's banging off this headboard! You're hurting me.'
     'Sorry.'

I'll be the first to *really* do it. No talk, no dreaming, only creation, action! I'll not wait. I'll make *everything* happen. Oh, what about Suzie? She needs freed, from Frank, she deserves it. Can I do everything? Yeah, I can, I can do anything! Want to explode out of myself now! Come on, want to start everything! Wow, the brightness!

'OW! PAUL! JESUS!'
     'WHAT?'
     'My head! Look! I'm BLEEDING!'
     'Oh god.'
     'Stop FUCKING ME! Come OUT!'
     'Right!'
     'God, someone's coming in! Pull out!
     'Okay!'

Shit! Going to come! Can't stop it! Where're my clothes? Door's opening! Sperm's rising. There it goes…oh, very bland, that's surprising…and some staff

67

member's walked in wearing a yellow jacket. Or maybe it's golden.

'So sorry to barge in, we did try phoning and no one answered the door…oh, I'll turn around, so sorry to walk in at this moment, we…'

Jan's hiding under the quilt. Camera's still bleeping. Staff member's turned around. I should ask what's going on, but I won't. Wait for him to speak, get your cords on.

'Yes, I'm sorry, but the room next door's filled with smoke. It's under control but we couldn't use the alarm as it's been damaged. Some neds threw a smoke bomb device in the window. There's a lot of smoke, and some bricks wrapped in…'

Oh, I can say something. So say it then. Now!

'Were they wrapped in newspaper and shit?'
    'Yes sir, they were. Have you…'
    'There was a similar incident at the university library.'
    'Oh'
    'Were the bricks wrapped in tabloids or broadsheets?'
    'Tabloids.'
    'Yes, thought so.'
    'Yes, right, so if you could please make your way down to the…'

His voice is diminishing. They all do eventually. Oh, feel every muscle pulsing. Energised, committed. Brilliant. Ambience in this room's crisper. Back's curving with power. Phone's humming in my pocket. A message:

C u @ 9 @ mill. Rembr £.

Oh yeah! Drink…good idea. Look, Jan's head's appeared. Spots of blood on her forehead. She looks concerned; talking to the man in the coat of gold.

'And can I ask…what message did they spray on the revolving door?'
   'A few letters on each window, spelling out…ahem…*fuck hotels.*'

Ha!

12

Love this place! Iron pillars, curved roof, old brick, red lighting: a Victorian factory, now a club with themes. Genius! Factory machine parts made into tables with black candles in bottles. Occult images on walls alongside Victorian photographs of the masses trooping out factory gates; some tinted red. What meaning, what confusion! What *is* the darkest force? God, backbone is solid with electricity! Stop and think. Is it a satanic influence over mankind, the factory owners, the working class masses? Wow.

There's an oversized image of shawl - wearing women, toothless men with bonnets, sooty jackets, children without shoes, flooding streets with collectivism. No individual's different. How horrific: bred into crowds without dreams. Anger, acceptance, spread like sexual disease. They got it wrong! They were always wrong! Frank's wrong!

Next to it's a photograph taken from a high vantage point of a man made up like Satan. Red skin, yellow eyes, horned forehead, black suit. Smiling, standing unnoticed, among city workers in a busy city square. Love it! Yeah, he's willing us to succeed. Ha! Forget about being human. We're pure dynamism, atoms. Faithless! Great! Should write this down. Come on!

Wait! There's another photograph. A suited man by a fireplace, pipe hanging from moustachioed mouth. A woman's seated in a corner with well-dressed children at her feet. Behind the man is a crucifix on the wall, next to a painting of a factory complex. There's a small engine on a table. Caption under the photograph reads "Victorian Industrialist and Inventor with Family". He's the energy of the family, of industry. Motivator of the middle classes, empire, battery of the world! But there's fear in his eyes. Of what? Himself, communism, his family, Satan? Cool, oh it's so cool.

His expression's like dad's. Dad's face was connected to some magnet that stopped him being human. Cunt.

Mum: took me on random trips, dragged me out of school, made an excuse, to look at rocks with ancient designs, sunny days, air, wind, her old camera...oh, there's Ian, under the photograph, drinking a bottle of something. Orange glint across the bottom of my eyes there.

'Hi Ian.'

'Paul. Where've you been?'

'I was starring in a porn film but the hotel was attacked by mysterious urban terrorists.'

'You're a strange bastard. What made you think of that?'

'It's true.'

'Come on, get the drinks in. You'd better stick to coke; your face looks like it's twisted.'

'No, I need vodka. I'm buzzing. It'll calm me down. Honest.'

'Mmm, alright. Let's grab a seat at the bar.'

Red lights soften Ian's face. There's a smile, could mean anything in this atmosphere. Women keep passing us, going to the toilets on the left there. Expensive clothing, magazine skin, long bodies. Air sizzles silver around them. Can't stop rubbing my crotch against the bar.

'I've got a collection now.'

'Right. Of what?'

'Property details, for Brighton, you dozy twat. Haven't you been listening?'

'Yeah, yeah!'

'Christ! You really need to get off them meds. Look, there're tons of opportunities. The market's right.'

'For shops?'

'For shops, flats, supplies, anything. Everything's coming down in price.'

'Right.'

His chin's curling again.

'So, you told Mandy you're buying down south then?'

'Not yet. It's complicated.'

'Why?'

His face's stopped, just stopped being a face…now he's back. What happened there?

'Mandy's got other plans. I've told you, she's staying here for Karl. I'm not part of the picture…that's it. But there's…unfinished business.'

'Oh right.'

'You can't rely on women. You can't. Nothing's stable. Your ex wife was the same.'

Kate! Oh my god, Kate!

Kate, what happened to you? I didn't like your mottled tits but you've gone! A mother. Wendy's mother! That's why I don't remember. You hated me after Wendy, blamed me.

I hated me after Wendy. Now don't start with this. But she'd be at school now, going to birthday parties, staying over at friends, writing in her diary, hiding in her room. What could I do though? No, it *was* my fault.

Stop it! Have to fight this off. Oh…well, that was easy. Wonder if it's the meds. Feels like they're working. There's a woman over there in a thin golden blouse, her nipples are shimmering beneath, like medals for me.

'Ian, I want to go to Brighton with you. I've got plans.'
    'I don't know if that's a smart idea.'
    'It's a perfect idea. We can be partners.'
    'You'd need money Paul.'
    'I've got collateral.'
    'That caravan you disappeared to after Kate? It's barely standing.'

Bastard! That's right! Couldn't deal with the Kate thing, so bought a stationary caravan, at 'Bourne Caravan Park' just north of Fairfields. Moved in for three weeks of darkness, fog, hate, masturbation. Nothing. No one knew. Drained myself of everything. Became a capable human. Became me.

'I'll get something for it. I've got savings. I'd get a job in a library, do a business masters.'
    'Paul, I don't know what's going to happen. Everything's fucked up mate.'
    'It's easy. Let's go. Check out some premises. Brochures are fine, but you need to look around, touch it, smell it. Tomorrow, after work.'
    'Calm down cousin. We can't just take off.'
    'Yeah, we *can.*'
    'I need to sort things out with Mandy. Then I'll make a move. Just need to make sure she knows…exactly where I stand.'
    'Thought you said you couldn't rely on women? Just leave her.'
    'I know. But I…'
    There's another smile. Don't want to know what it

means. Probably something emotional. Need to get him focused. Look at that woman there, legs so smooth they look produced. Wonder if I can…'

'Paul!'

'What?'

'You're drifting. Stick with the plot!'

'What *is* the plot? Nothing's happening! Come *on* Ian!'

'Will you calm down, you psycho? I'll make a move soon. Look, let's get some more in, then buy some bottles, go back to yours. I'm tired.'

'Okay.'

13

…and now we have a classic for you, a song so evocative of warm nights, romance and the loss of innocence, a Bobby Goldsboro hit, Summer (the First Time)…enjoy…

…wait…Someone's trying the door. People coming in! Voices! No, one voice, sounds like Ian but drunk, all hiss like the radio. I must have been, no, *he* must have been with Ian then. Ian never drinks without me, maybe he needs me sometimes but I can drink without him, without anyone. Maybe I, maybe *he* passed out, gave Ian my key, but what for? Have I given him everything, again, like last summer? But I've given nothing to anyone, have I, only money, and a motorbike, once.

The door's opening and there's Ian, pulling something…oh god…he's dragging *him* into the lounge, by my coat, can hear him grunt, sucking saliva, I'm a cunt, do I sound like that? A fish noise and Kate me made sleep in the livingroom. Poor Kate. No, fuck Kate.

Ian looks sober, so why is *he* so pissed? The meds, never drink on a trial, dehydration could lead to 'toxicity', doctor says, but I've done it again, no, *he's* done it. Look, his face's slipping.

Ian's lifting him onto the futon, he's strong, always has been, never twitched when uncle Philippe died, saw his eyes, at the funeral, his grin that meant everyone was mad apart from him so why am I like this then? Can't control anything, there're piss stains on my, on *his* cords. Could be dying, alcohol and meds, reacted inside, but if he dies, will I? But he *is* me.

Is this permanent? Yes? I deserve this. Freedom's not real, I've looked, tried, there's nothing there, there's nothing here…I've got radio though, got space, this corner…I *am* space then, but no direction, the only thing to care about, is it, but there's nothing I can do. How can I move? Don't blame me, no one can move me, no escape…*stop*.

Aw…Ian is sitting by my body on the futon; he's never been so close and the atoms are interested, rushing through our bodies, dragging colours, blues, purples, slithers from Ian's forehead but he doesn't feel anything though; he's sitting, staring at the floor and…something's happening, look.

Pixels lifting in one rainbow buzz…the vampire cloud of our colours…what're they…rushing towards the wall and…What an explosion, didn't know they could be so dynamic like that.

Debris settling, aah, lulling like summer insects, but making a picture, very fluid. This is real art, isn't it? Eric was wrong, he said art had to be created and he hand-printed t-shirts and sold them on a stall but art's there all the time. What did I do to you Eric? I wrote a bad review of your band's demo, they were called 'Maze', in the student paper, our final year, and why did I do that? You were my friend and you had OCD, but no one sees art, Eric, because it keeps changing; I can't even see Ian now, my body, futon, room, all drowned by moving colour and I could die now, it's okay, and everything's changed into…what is it?

I know this place…It's the living room of Barnaby Cottage, our first home, rented from a farmer with Alzheimer's, for me, Kate, Wendy, when I was someone else…oh god no, couldn't bear seeing…is she there…no, it's me, look, in shadow, and this is like I'm watching an episode from a soap, with me in it. I'm a camera up in the corner, watching me sitting on an old wooden chair. An old wooden chair…what a calming phrase and Kate collected them from dumps, they knew her there, and second-hand shops, so many and we had to throw them out, didn't we, paint some, or kill them for firewood, falling over them, sitting on them till they snapped. I remember the chairs.

The living room was dark though, even during the day when I was alone with Wendy. It was hidden behind trees in a lane, behind Upton Mews and the windows were small, it had a low roof but we used candles until Wendy started crawling, see, we had space for our child, little lights in little windows, an anti-city life, something like that and I painted the walls purple, door handles silver, see what you did for them Paul.

I was good, can't remember, but I *must* have been, you couldn't talk to me anyway, Kate, I can't remember you but Wendy loved me so I *must* have been good, see. My child put her arms out for me and smiled; she drew pictures with my face in them, wasn't there one on the fridge and you never smiled, Kate. I don't want to remember you.

But you made bread Kate, I remember that, but I couldn't eat it, and you ran a dollhouse shop with your schizophrenic mum, in Upton Mews. What is it now, a property shop probably, but no dolls for me because I was an English student, with no parents, working in the library part-time and it sounds alright when you think in sentences like this, doesn't it? Everything's okay here, isn't it?

But my face there, look at it, so black it's hard to see but bits are reflected in glass tears and white metal, over the scarlet rug beside the open fire, all bits of a mirror I'd smashed with a toaster, an engagement present from Ian but it stopped working, everything always does and I threw it, I had to, against everything. But you didn't keep these things from me Kate. Why didn't you understand, protect me? Why didn't you read the book, mania, liable to 'explosiveness', ...Oh, here comes Kate now with a dollhouse roof under her doll's arm. She'll probably question me, didn't trust me.

She always smiled first though, one that meant she was managing, look, she's doing it now, she won't breakdown, never, but it's different when you see it like this, in a repeat but it wasn't my fault if she didn't manage, was it? I couldn't so...

Her hair makes her look stressed, that's all, nothing to worry about, is it? That blonde mess on her head, trapped with pins and other things, but escaping or maybe it's her eyes, yes, they were too small for her, well that's what it is then. Makes her look affected by something and...Stop it, she didn't care, with that white face, that small stare.

No, but everyone said Kate was doing *so* well! Oh it was such a *difficult* birth, she lost a lot of blood, oh yes, the poor woman's hormones must have shorted, her nerve endings grated but she's *wonderful* with little Wendy. Funny how we cope, isn't it and she will be *fine*, of course she will.

She's staring at the floor now, the mirror, bashed toaster, me, it's not good so can I leave and her teeth are showing, her chalk gums, gothic lips dragged down and she's about to murmur. She never shouted at me, why would she? She loved me, she said that once, did she say that? Can never remember what you said, Kate and you're all foggy now, milky but we have this repeat though; there you are, unfocused. Look, you're talking now:

'Why've you smashed the mirror and toaster?'
  'Sorry, what was that? You'll have to speak up.'
  'Why have you…I said why've you done this?'

Is that what she said? Could never hear her. She's trying to be calm and her face is so small and did she always tremble like that but that wasn't me, was it?

'Oh right…well, I lost control. The fucking toaster stopped working.'
  'Did you *have* to do this?'

Did she really ask that? Why didn't she know? Why did everything have to be explained and did her eyes always look pink and did I really look at her like that?

'No I didn't, true, but why the fuck is every simple thing so FUCKING COMPLICATED!? I ONLY WANTED A PIECE OF TOAST!'
  'Where's Wendy?'
  'What!'
  'I said, where's our baby?'

Yeah, where is she, oh god, can't see her, glad I can't, don't want to but she's probably sleeping, that's all, little baby, in the cot next door, playing with your mobile, plastic giraffes on strings and your moon nightlight, your face lilac. And you hummed when you slept, like you were singing and I laughed when I watched you sleep once, that's all she's doing Kate, sleeping, her afternoon nap. But Kate's going over to the window, her hands covering her mouth, no don't. She's gone outside, but there's Ian, at the living room door. Yes, come on in Ian! He'll say something and Kate hated him but we all need Ian, don't we? Come in

Ian!

Oh, that was quick, that's good, she's back with Wendy in her arms. Oh Wendy, oh no, daddy will...she's two years old, only a baby and her face is so...pink, wide eyes, open mouth, curled hair everywhere and daddy knows where you've been! In the garden again with your nappy at your knees, looking at flowers and slugs and dead bees and butterflies oh and look, your vest is stained, you're all wet! Have you been playing in puddles again, let daddy...She was curious Kate, that's all, liked to play in the garden, daddy lets you, so what's wrong Kate? You're so quiet, don't say anything then, say *something* Ian.

'Oh, toaster fucked then?'
    'Yeah, couldn't fix it Ian. Lost it a bit, you know.'
    'Well, what can you do, eh? It was cheap.'
    'Yeah. Ah, so *there* you are Wendy, been in the garden *again* sweetheart?'

Kate must hate me; want to kill me, but she's silent. I like silence but nobody's moving in the film now. It's stopped. What...and now everything's swelling out! Can't we stop for a minute and Kate's face, it's in the middle of the wall, Wendy's head's under her chin and Kate's close-up is still expanding! Stop!

Look at Kate's eyes! I can't turn away, no escaping them, jerking, veins like scars, look, grey swirl behind her pupils but I've never had a close-up before so how could I have known.

I can't do anything, where can I go, can't go anywhere. What did I do then? I was reading Shelley, I had to, they, no *she* wouldn't talk to me anyway, wouldn't touch me when I was lying awake in the dark in that living room on a broken bed-settee, hearing her breathe next door, Wendy dreaming, I was living alone, they weren't there.

That face is...still now. But there're lumps under her skin, moving, no, rising, from out of her face. Separating from her. Floating, in front. The tiny grains, look, oh thank god, she's dissolving.

But there's black left behind, from where dots have drifted, like pepper, and is this what memory does, leave holes in the present, but can see the room coming back: futon, Ian and me. And there I am, still out of it, on the futon and Ian's looking up here, at me! Wonder if...Ian! Ian! Come on! See me! No, hear me, come *on*...

Nothing. Wait......why are you sobbing like that? What's wrong with you cousin? I've never seen you weep. You didn't cry at uncle Phillip's funeral, neither did I, or mum's, but now there's snot over your lips, your eyes are leaking but they shouldn't be, come on Ian, don't look up here like that, I haven't done anything, what will we do if you...

14

Should phone in sick. But need to speak to Christine. Make plans. Drop the library idea. Want to move…to Brighton. Settle there. Take Christine. Screw Suzie in her allotment first. Writhe in her cabbages. Wreck Frank's life. Everything's clearer, nearly. Head's squeezed though. Stop complaining. Ask Christine out to dinner today. Explain everything.

Ian must've left before me then. Probably in the shop by now. So he missed the neighbours, this morning ritual. Love watching them stride towards their cars. Power on private streets. Air clear around them, but lemon, faded documentary light. Bleeping things, real adults. Polite chatter, hate and fear. And off they go to make money. Socialism will never work. Frank's an idiot.

Eric was a socialist until his depressed girlfriend dumped him and his band, 'Maze', broke up. Then he was a capitalist. Selling t-shirts on a stall in the mall. Probably felt alternative. Fairytale creatures on cheap cotton? Not proper capitalism though, is it? But he probably leaves early in the morning. Sets up his stall, makes money. Just like them.

Frank has to be a socialist. I've never asked. The bastard. Want to hate Frank more though; this isn't enough…but something's capping it. That thing… what is it…oh yeah…guilt. How did that happen then? What've I done now? Nothing. I think. So why am I…something must've happened last night. A guilt inducing barbiturate, dropped into my vodka. It'll wear off.

Meeting the doctor today, last thing. His special 'early evening slot'. Just for me. For a review of the meds. Well, they've blocked a depressive episode. The medications have engendered 'an antidepressant effect'. Sounds like a good thing to say. Probably negate a lot of talk. Good. What else can I say…thinking is more structured? Yes, sounds positive, plans forming. Oh, there goes a blue spark, in the sink water. Still getting visuals then, not much else though.

Not so many students waiting outside the library this morning. Only women. Demure and juvenile. Soft clothes, therapy voices, doctor smiles. Professional already. Suits the charcoal sky above them. Greyness curling down too, licking the library door. Can I deal with mist today? I can do anything. Fuzz in the head? Tingle in the wrist? Psychosomatic, that's all. But I'm not here anyway. I'm ahead. This won't trap me. Ah, here comes old John with Christine.

There're perfect swellings of flesh, probably untouched, beneath Christine's tweed. Look at her, under library lights, tits casting shadows over her torso. She's coming towards me. Her citrus smile. Here it comes, her hand on my arm.

'How are you this morning, Paul? You look very…weary.'

    'I'm fine. Is the smoke damaged section open yet?'

    'Not yet. It'll take a few weeks. Graffiti's gone though, cleaned off.'

    'Who did it?'

    'Two youths, apparently, although the CCTV footage is inconclusive.'

    'Right. You don't look so stressed today anyway, Christine.'

'Really? Did I look stressed before?'

Can see Christine sitting beside me on a train. She leans on me and sleeps. Telephone poles and fields fly past the window. Pink light from the setting sun on her face. We don't know where we're going. We don't care. We could do anything, go...

'Well, you looked...I've got an idea, did I tell you? For a novel! It's already written, in my head.'

'A novel? Why not tell me about it over lunch? I've got a lot to be...'

'In the Union? Can't stand the food there.'

'Oh well.'

I'll write in a study. In the evenings. In a Victorian flat with original cornices, in Brighton. Gustav Klimt on the lime wall. High ceiling. One novel a year. Think about a creative writing masters after the first 'critically acclaimed' work. Christine will work in another library and carry on with her PhD. We'll fuck every morning and...

'Right, well, why not meet up somewhere else, for dinner, tonight? I'd love your opinion on this. This novel's important to me.'

'Ah...tell you what, speak to me later, before you leave, I have to go and...'

'Okay. I'll be in the Upton Arms at eight, tonight.'

'So...ah...there's a team meeting at ten. Please come along, there'll be biscuits. Bye for now.'

She's *so* compressed! All that passion, layered, ready to be relieved! Edges of her body threatened! Intense! *Have* to see her naked! Have to think of an idea for a novel! Fuck!

15

Community Lounge looks different today. Probably the mist. Upton Mews looks old in mist. Fairfields looks blank. Numbing. But there's something on the lounge window, new graffiti. Have to get closer. In bright pink, it says 'FUCK POVERTY'! And there's a crack in the wooden door, shit on the pavement beside a newspaper page with a bingo advertisement. Ha! It's a campaign! This is organised! Action in Fairfields? Wow.

What am I doing here today anyway? Smoke a fag. Watch violet worms zip away into nothing. Where do they go? Want to follow them. Spine is pushing me to follow. None of this is real. It's in the past already. Present makes me want to vomit. Slit my…here comes Frank. Didn't know he smoked.

'Alright there, Paul?'
 'Afternoon Frank. I didn't know you smoked.'
 'Only two a day, mate, only two a day.'

Who smokes two fags a day? Freak!

Got my first fag from a pervert. Dad bought mum a new stereo after her first suicide attempt. It was huge. I took polystyrene from the box it came in and built a chair from it on a piece of wood. Floated down Quarry Burn in it. Sank near Black Cliffs, under a disused Victorian viaduct. Nearly drowned. Crawled out and hid under an arch. An old man was there. He smelt of dogs and urine. There were empty bottles and burnt mattresses. He gave me a fag and lit it. Asked me to come and share his sleeping bag with him, until I dried. Dirty air blew into the arch.

'Got them research questions here, mate. You up for it?'

'The research…oh yeah. How many participants?'

'Dunno. Hard to tell, mate. We've publicised; it's all we can do. You'll probably get two punters, maybe three. I'll show them through to the Community Suite, tell them to wait for you.'

'So, I go through these questions with them and…'

'Yeah, they'll get vouchers for doing it. Pete put it on the fuckin' posters.'

'Vouchers for what?'

'Mobile phone credit, what else?'

'Right. Any idea who sprayed this on the window?'

'Nope. CCTV camera was sprayed over, by two thin guys in hoodies and baseball caps. Couldn't make them out. Looks great though! Think we'll leave it there. What do you think?'

'Yeah, great!'

He doesn't get it! How can anyone be so submerged, not to see anything for what it is?

Oh god, look at these two, waiting for me. Two skeletons, in their thirties, rigid in office chairs, black tracksuits, white faces, open mouths, tramlines in short hair with baseball caps hiding pits in their skull. Uch! Do they really exist? Room looks criminal around them. Look, they're so televised. Can humans look televised? Course they can! This is Fairfields.

Calm the mirth, come on. Can't walk into the Community Suite and laugh! Can I? They look so suited to their roles though. Scripts scraped into card faces. I'm going to interview them. Record their thoughts. I'm a camera! Hey, but what's my name again? Oh god, quick…remember! Oh yeah, my name is Paul Belardo and I won't be here much longer. I'm leaving soon. And I'm a camera too.

Right, calm down, get in, interview them, get home and pack.

Doesn't feel right. They're answering questions in grunts. Mouth movement minimal. Think they're trying not to laugh. Why? I'm ridiculous to them. Fine. They're alien to me. I could never be so...*local*. Let them snigger in this lounge that's supposed to belong to them but they never use. Everything here begins with the word 'community'. A useless word. And this place smells like an old post office. Looks like a new tax office.

Every answer's a lie. This is a drama. They're performing for vouchers. But it's unconvincing. Can see their skin twitch like stage curtains. Something moving behind them, inside them. They're not real.

Maybe they know something. Whatever they know, it's irrelevant. Or maybe they know who sprayed on the window? Or did *they* do it? They fit the profile. Probably fit every profile. Improbable though; that would mean they'd have to know that something exists outside of Fairfields.

But look! There're splashes of colour on their trainers! So they adorn anything they pass with "fuck it" slogans? For what? To spread apathy, then home for chips and Methadone! Ha, the stupid...

'Yes, here are the vouchers. If you could just sign this...thank you so much for coming in this morning. This research is very important to us and we really appreciate you taking the time to talk to us. Yeah, thanks, take care, goodbye now.'

They bob out stiffly. Probably don't want to walk without seeming affected. Doorway seems harsher as they pass through it. Everything responds to contact with documentary extras. Sandpaper humans.

So they're pressured into vandalism through being confined? Frank's hopeless. It's obvious…they need liberated. Or lobotomised. Hah! Oh stop it now. No! This is fun! No one can hear, so what's the problem? People here have no idea of space. Give them space. Knock it all down. Spread them out. We should all live in fields.

We lived near a dairy for a while. Not far from Black Cliffs. A converted barn, one of the first. Rented. Lots of space there. Dad's idea: country lifestyle would help mum recover.

Did for a while. She baked, read, listened to the radio. Then it started again. Didn't care by that time.

Dad played ABBA music, sat by the fire, read British history magazines, played with a red byro in his hands. Mum wailed next door. Everything orange because the curtains were always closed; mum hated sunlight.

I wandered. Over fields, hills, anywhere. Found streams, dead animals, one girl my own age from Upton Mews.

I built a rocket from bins, broken pallets, stolen metal milk containers, planks of wood that smelt of shit. Stole it all from the dairy, stayed up all night to steal. I cried because it wouldn't work. Sat in it for hours. Went home for tea and then came back and sat in it until suppertime.

Got in the rocket one morning, found the school report card I'd hidden in my bedroom. The one that detailed my 'bemusing rebelliousness'. Went home with it. Dad stared at me, looked hurt, hummed something in Spanish, took tea through to mum in her room, then sat by the fire with a book on Scottish castles and a red pen. I wandered until we moved back into Curby city. I know space.

Dad suffered. That's all he did. Why did he do that for her? You kept trying, it never worked dad. Why did you not leave then? Oh dad.

What? I didn't think that…ah, it's an 'intrusive thought'. The 'distressing' thoughts that are not intended, I'm accepting that the thought exists doctor, then disregarding it and I'm doing well.

Oh look, here comes Pete. Come on in Pete. Let me see you shuffle. Can smell you already, that untreated working class sweat. Now you're grinning. Not the usual smirk though. Almost a smile. But they never work with greasy hair, Pete. And here it is, one cough, then the sawdust rasp. Oh, he's going to speak to me. There's no one else in here. Oh my god!

'Yeah, alright Paul. Got the results then?'
    'Results? What results?'
    'The research. With the…'
    'Oh yeah. Yes, it's here, nothing extraordinary.'
    'Right then. Can I get it then?'
    'Why?'
    'Frank wants *me* to collate the results. Organise them, with the other results, for that MEP bloke. We're passing the research on. The guy's interested.'
    'What? Where's Frank?'
    'He's popped out. Fuckin' 'ell! Just give me the fuckin' results! Fucksake!'
    'Here, take them, Christ!'
    'Right then!'

89

Frank's been encouraging him. Why? He needs reconditioned first. Ah, my novel's hero maybe? That's it! Overcoming tragedy, yeah, from damp bedsit with one bar fire to socialist god with hygiene issues! Grab a pen. Quick! When can I leave? When can I leave this job, leave everything?

Leave now! No, can't. But stomach's cramping for it, Jesus! Lounge's even changing colour. Tinted yellow now. Looks better, older. Go out, come on, smoke a fag instead then. Phone's vibrating.

'Hello?'

'It's Jan. You busy later?'

'I've got an appointment at six.'

'Come to the house at five then.'

'Okay.'

The house? In daylight hours? Must be important.

16

Jan's dressed like a wife. Some reflective top, low cut thing. Far too sitcom-ish. It's confusing me. Is her husband due home? Someone else's in the lounge. Can hear them pouring a drink. I need a theme tune here…

'Come through here Paul; there's someone I'd like you to meet.'

Jan has friends? Never thought of that. Or maybe he's home, in there, waiting to confront me. Or congratulate me. I've been used. To invigorate their sex life...his hairy, grey back, her chemical smell, this childless house. A dry marriage. So fuck.

I'm in the living room. Had to take my shoes off. Never been in here before. Looks like a successful golfer's home. Pictures of putting greens, massive plasma television, white carpet, white furniture, pale yellow walls, glass-topped coffee table. Nothing surprising. Apart from that woman standing there. Or is she standing in the corner? How many of them are there? One. Thank god. What happened there?

'Paul, I'd look you to meet Penny, Penny Dawn. Penny owns the digital hire shop, remember?'
    'Oh yeah…hello Penny.'
    'Hi Paul.'
    They sit down next to each other on the leather settee like twins. Penny has a scruffiness that means she's far too nice but would get upset if you questioned why she's so happy. One of these balanced types, happy with their careers, life, vegetable patch, Sunday papers, large woollen jumpers, worn jeans, no make up, wild pubic hair. Smiles too much.

'Sit down Paul; you're in time for the premier. Penny's done a lot of work on this. She's so clever.'

'Oh, okay…great.'

I'm being directed to this large chair. Why this ceremony? I float around this house, never touch anything. Never sit, never have time. She's trying to impress Penny. Pretend we have an adult relationship. Should I call her 'darling' then?

Wonder if this is where her husband sits? There's a dimple in the leather on the left arm, probably where he rests his whisky when he's home. Must need alcohol after arguing with Europeans. There's a button there on the…should I…yes, a foot rest!

'Oh…comfortable Paul? I'll press play, shall I? You ready, Penny?'

'Ha, yeah, go for it Jan!'

You can't tell it's me. Can see the back of my head, yeah, but my hair looks darker. Didn't realise I had ripples moving down my back like that when I moved. God, my arse's so lifeless…nothing but skin, creasing, animal hide and grease.

Penny *is* clever. Scene looks shaded by something. More dramatic. No sound at all. She's done something else, the screen jerks. An illusion of movement for drama. Expect the police to burst in soon and…of course, I see what she's done, because in comes the hotel guy…now! Ha! I turn around, an expression of shock, I didn't even mean it, and the film ends. Perfect. A black screen. The hotel guy could have been anyone! It's a dirty little film!

'So, what do you think Paul?'

'Yeah, it's good Jan. Penny's done well with it.'

I've been copied! Now I'm also on screen. An electric double made up of pixels. A mystery man in a porn film. Maybe I'll be seen by people I'll never meet. They'll masturbate while they watch me.

I masturbated in the toilets in the maternity wing. Kate was in labour with Wendy. Wing was busy with lunches being taken into a ward. Had to rush to the toilets. Saw a sweaty teen, maybe eighteen, visiting her friend. Passed her on the way to the unit. She was bending over a cot, looking at her friend's baby, with these tits, puberty fresh, pink with hospital flush, escaping from a summer top.

White walls in the cubicle were stained. Probably by other horny fathers-to-be. Heard someone in another cubicle moaning and thrashing. Tried to hurry, climax before he did, get out so he wouldn't see me. But we came at the same time. Washed my hands at the sink, thinking about being a brilliant dad from now on, showing everyone, especially Kate's mum who cried when the pregnancy was announced and threw a plate at me. I was going to build a cot.

I never built that cot. Katy really wanted…

Accept it, ignore it, and disregard it. So the other wanker came out too. He looked eighty years old, sweaty, pale, some new grandfather. Winked at me, punched his own chest. To restart his heart, probably. He complained about the standard of cleanliness. I've never wanked in a hospital again.

My porn image will survive me though. It'll live into science fiction. I should write about it. Screw the socialist hero idea! A novel, about my porn double, yeah, leaving the screen in 2115! Screwing sad housewives in therapeutic pods. I won't exist, but he'll have fun. I don't want to exist.

Jan's opening a bottle of champagne. That Penny woman's getting excited, clinking glasses, laughing like a girl with a high school secret, blood on toilet walls. And there's a chocolate cake. It should be brown, but it's too luminous. Something silver's exploding on the wall over there. What's the celebration for?

'Jan, why are we celebrating then?'

'Oh come on Paul! This film will free me!'

'Free you? How?'

'He'll divorce me after seeing this! Have some cake, but watch and not stain the chair. What do you think of the film?'

'Penny's done well, but I feel numb about it now, disconnected from my own...'

'Well it'll serve its purpose. He'll not have a choice now. It'll destroy him. Thank you for this, Penny.'

'Ha, not at all darling! Glad to help.'

'Well...here's to freedom! Paul, don't put your glass on the table.'

This place is too clean for parties. Can't wait to get home and...wonder if Ian will be there? Should I phone? No. He'll probably be back at Mandy's by now. He's a hypocrite; he could never live without a woman.

That Penny woman's holding Jan's hand. The happy types are always tactile. Kate hardly touched me. Right, I'm leaving; this is getting too nice. Doctor's waiting.

17

Does he realise how dated his certificates look? His desk lamp casts his shadow stain over them. Look like they belong on a church wall. There're words, symbols, glints. Some in red and gold font, unreadable in his catholic darkness.

Why does he display them? He's placed that desk lamp to cast a gothic double. Show his patients his power is sinister, justified.

Ha…he's too small for this. Clinical looking though. Eyes wet with concentration. Magnified by clear framed glasses that sparkle when he moves. You follow the light when he speaks. No choice. Room dulls around him. I hate evening sessions.

Now he's going to ask questions. Scan me for imperfections. Then he writes them down, words like 'mania' and 'rapid cycling', I've had 'four or more episodes a year', enabled his diagnosis. And I'm packaged away until next time. He's so neat. Feel tucked in when I leave.

'So, Paul, have you noticed any significant effects since beginning this trial? Any…new symptoms, sudden mood swings, hallucinations at all?

Have fallen asleep at unusual times. Woken up somewhere new, in the middle of something, forgotten how I got there, why I was doing what I was doing. And that guilt from nowhere. He'd categorise it if I told him. I like it though.

And there're the sparks. But aren't they always there? Can't remember and…and difficulty concentrating. Again, that's common. Wanting to leave my body, fuck off somewhere, do something amazing?

Everyone feels like that, surely. Constant erection? Don't tell him; he'd take it away.

'No, no effects to report.'

'Right…excellent. So, have any suicidal thoughts returned during the trial at all? Have you felt any urge for escape?'

Kate phoned me and told me she was leaving. That's all she said. Didn't say where. Don't know why she phoned. Been apart for months. She'd never phoned before. First phone call I'd had in the flat. Rang like an alarm.

One sentence, then silence. I didn't believe her. Then she left. She must have phoned from the train station.

She'd always been practical. Probably consulted a timetable. Never let anyone down, even her inner command. I bought my stationary caravan that afternoon.

There was a paragraph in the local paper a week later. Some kid saw Kate, standing on the tracks, waiting for the express. She looked at her. Both caught in that vacuum between life and death. The child was four. She said Kate's face was blank, before she screamed and dived on the tracks. But she climbed onto the platform, seconds before the train passed. Got onto a train headed to Glasgow five minutes later. Maybe she's still there.

She never loved me. I didn't love her. We had a kid, but she kept her from me. Slept with her in our bed so I couldn't get in. Played with her apart from me. I heard them laugh through the wall. Let me study though.

She never cared. When I was diagnosed she took Wendy and lived with her mum for eight weeks. Said she needed her support. When she returned her face was tight. Eyes like stones. She'd always had that face. Always yearning for that train.

Oh Kate. I never did anything to help you, did I, but how could I, you would never have let me near, I was too extreme, you said, but I was stressed, you knew that, but you wouldn't...

Intrusive, accepted, ignored. Did the doctor hear that? No, how can he? Could he see it on my face though? Jesus, if anyone could see that...say something, he's looking concerned.

'No, no suicidal thoughts at all. Although I would like to move, begin a masters course, but not escape.'
    'Okay. You look confused, Paul. Are you okay?'
    'Yes, of course, I'm fine.'
    'Alright. Have you brought along your mood chart today?'
    'Yes, it's in here...oh no, wait...oh, I'm sorry, it appears I've left it at home.'
    'Never mind. Perhaps you could talk through some of your recent mood cycles.'

Knew he was going to say that.

'Paul, it's very important to record your moods during this trial. This medication is still at the research stage. You are one of only sixty trialists worldwide. However, in a few cases in America the drug did induce psychosis, or longer periods of mania.'
    'That's very interesting doctor. However, I can assure you that this drug has been effective in stemming an imminent episode of depression. I feel normal. I've suffered no hallucinations, no mania. I've been enjoying an extended period of normalcy.'

'Good, but if…it would be more prudent for me to come to a conclusion about the effectiveness of your medications based on an analysis of your feelings, which would require more detail from you, Paul.'

We always do this. Words spark from us like energy, no real meaning. Wish I could stop my legs from jerking. He'll notice.

'I agree doctor. I can provide you with an overview. Would that suffice?'
     'It would be a beginning, Paul.'
     'Since our last meeting I've noticed a significant difference in my perception.'
     'Can you elaborate?'
     'I can plan, structure my thoughts around single ideas, perceive of logical projections from a base point. I enjoy clarity of visualisation.'

That was *good*.

'Okay Paul. Is this the only development?'
     'Yes.'
     'Okay…I'm concerned that you're reflections are not revealing as much as they could. Can I be honest Paul…there's no point in us…well, you look very tired and you seem intensely distracted this evening. Your face is red and your eyes are glazed. I feel it would be beneficial to…'
     'Before I came here I went to the gym in the city centre. Got straight into a taxi after an hour on a treadmill. Honestly. I want to ensure my body enjoys my renaissance too.'

Enjoy my renaissance? I like it. But he's right though. I'm distracted. Film running in the back of my head.

Fantasy home movie. Christine and I, naked, wet, playing with each other in my dark caravan. Rain stabbing the roof. Fog in the corners. Who's filming us? I should hire Penny! And Suzie walks in. Sweating, wiping earth from her hard body! Her vagina has grass in it. Things start to…

'Paul, I'd like to ensure that you understand the potentially negative effects of this medication. I don't want to scare you, or dissuade you from remaining on the trial. The side effects I'm referring to are very rare indeed. Rather, I'd like to talk through some reported symptoms, to inform you, that's all.'

'Of course. Please, go ahead.'

'A trialist in America reported a long psychotic episode. In fact, the patient was affected for a month. The psychosis was severe; the patient was convinced that a previously unknown place existed within his home behind a door that shifted to elude him.'

'Interesting. I can assure you that I know my flat's geography. What happened to the…trialist?'

'The patient knocked a hole in his wall. He wanted to find this phantom space, where he was sure others were watching him.'

'Was anyone there…no, sorry, stupid question.'

'No. However, the trialist was sectioned. Unfortunately, he committed suicide.'

'Oh.'

'You see, the drug can engender significant paranoia, psychosis and delusions if any early symptoms of these side effects are not recorded and acted upon. I repeat, these symptoms are rare in the extreme, but we still need to be vigilant.'

'I have nothing to report. No one is watching me in my home, doctor. My thoughts have even been free of negativity since I took the first tablet. I can physically feel my whole system rejuvenate. Purpose has returned to my thinking.'

'Okay Paul. Please, record your thoughts and moods over the next few weeks and try to be as accurate and as honest as you can. We have to be methodical if this trial is to be successful. Is there anything you would like to ask me?'

'No, I'm happy with this trial so far. See you in a few weeks, Doctor.'

If I don't screw somebody now, my balls are going to explode! Christine will turn up tonight. So get in the pub early then, have a few drinks, calm this erection.

18

Smells like a furniture showroom in here. Not good for a bar and diner, is it? That's what the sign says now, 'Upton Mews Bar and Diner'. Music's inconsequential. Think it's Queen, but their eighties period. Place has the atmosphere of a hotel lobby. Bar staff have matching uniforms. Red shirts, blouses, black ties, black trousers and skirts. Here comes one now. Are they meant to look like Italian Fascists? Will they kill me? Will I kill me? Stop it!

'What can I do for you this evening, sir?'
    'Vodka and coke, no ice please.'

Where's Christine? Why's this place so spacious? What have they done now? How can walls disappear, buildings remain? These people must be supporting it with their guts. Eating, wedged in wooden chairs around wooden tables. Furniture's too pure to be real.
    All these families, mist of crimson above them. That's new, like blood cells suspended. And look at their eyes. Wide when they laugh at nothing.
    This is display eating. Who can seem the happiest? Which is the most bonded carnivore unit? They're tribal. It's horrific.
    And over there, sitting at the bar, women with scarves bought on holiday. Shiny things flashing in mature hair. Perfected hand movements. Jangles with bangles. Evening masks. Professional grins. Minds nestled in permanence. Golden colour trying to exist there under pink lights.
    Like these middle-aged men at the fruit machine with golf jumpers. Ironed trousers, polished shoes, contentment. Is that Eric with them? Can't be. Is it?

Unless he's got a mortgage now, savings, right wing philosophy. Capitalism has changed him then. No more denim coats and Genesis t-shirts. Looks like a real adult now. He's wearing a shirt and tie. Even his glasses are more mature. Probably has a people-carrier.

Stop looking over there. He'll want to come over. Blame me for things. Oh good, his face is blending with the others, into one adult. Thank god I'm mad.

Christine's got half an hour, and I'm leaving.

Christine's forgotten. Or there's been another attack on the library. No, why target the library again? They've already fucked books. No, she's probably menopausal. Or she fears me. I'm too intense. But why flirt if...ah, she's fearful of *herself*, not me. Like these cunts! All dressed to...wait...that's Suzie over there, in the lounge bar! Yes!

'Hi Suzie, can I get you a drink?'
    'Lager, pint of.'
    'Okay. So, how are you, how's Frank?'
    'Frank's visiting his ex wife, again. Problems with the fuckin' kid. I don't matter tonight.'
    'Oh, right. What about you?'
    'I'm Suzie Hall. I'm dirty and worthless.'
    'I'm sure that's not true.'
    'Are you buying that lager?'

She is dirty though. Soil stains on bare arms. Flecks on her face. Damp patches on her black jeans and Whitesnake t-shirt. Hair scrambled by nature. Aroma of agriculture. God, why's she come in here then? To prove some point? No, she knew that I came in here, occasionally. She must have, that's why. Yes!

'Are you waiting for someone, Suzie?'

'Was Frank. Now it's god.'

'I stopped waiting.'

'You're not one of the chosen then.'

'What have you been chosen to do?'

'Suffer.'

'I'm sure that's not…'

'Where's that drink?'

'Ah, here it is.'

'So, do you still want me to mow your non-existent garden?'

'Oh, sorry about that. I wish I had a garden, you see.'

She's a martyr. I like martyrs. They're easy. What's she suffering for? Or who? Hope it's not Frank. She's too original. He couldn't match her scepticism. What could he offer her anyway? A social conscience? Wouldn't work.

Ian sacrificed himself for Mandy. I told him that. He met her at college. She worked in the canteen, sang along to songs on the radio. Breasts sagging in white uniform. After three months, he moved in with her and her son, who began bedwetting.

We were outside Fairfields post office, next to Jan's chemist's, waiting for it to open. That's when I told him. Ian wanted a brochure he'd ordered on business properties in the south. It was icy. An old woman slipped, wailed on the pavement. Her handbag skimmed under a car. I told Ian he should stop dreaming now he'd moved in with Mandy. She'd drag him down, into comfort. He punched me, ran off. The old woman answered a mobile phone that was humming in her pocket.

Jan must have heard something. She came out,

looked at me, the old woman. First time we'd met. The old woman moaned, hid her mobile. Jan titled her head at me, sloth-like. She offered the old woman a hand. There was a gold pool on the pavement where she'd fallen. The old woman mocked amnesia, tottered into the post office. Jan asked me into the chemist's. 'You're bleeding', she said. Her first words to me. My blood dripped onto her white blouse, under her lab coat. Trickled towards her tits. We fucked that night. Her husband wasn't home.

Surely Suzie's not succumbed to a relationship? Test her out then. Ask her why she's suffering.

'Suzie, why are you suffering?'
    'I suffer because nothing changes.'
    'You're waiting for God to explain?'
    'I'll suffer until she does.'

Don't know if I like this. Yeah, she's bitter. I like that. Philosophical, but childish. Too general. Can predict her answers. Try something else.

'Have you noticed the fuck-everything graffiti?'
    'No.'
    'They spray fuck-everything slogans on buildings and throw bricks through windows and smoke bombs, more of a symbolic bomb probably. The bricks are covered in shit and wrapped in newspapers.'
    'Are they?'
    'They did it to Fairfields Community Lounge.'
    'What did they spray?'
    'Fuck poverty.'
    'Boring though, isn't it?'
    'Exactly!'

Oh god, she's not getting it. Can't bear seeing congratulatory expressions on stupid people!

'Yeah, that's right, boredom; the graffiti is a city-wide attempt to make us think differently, to make us think like them.'

'Like who? What are you talking about?'

'The vandals, from the scheme. They're trying to smash middle class perception. Poison middle class culture with fatalism. They've hit a university library, a hotel, a charity funded by professionals to *help* them. If everything's worthless, we're worthless. Things would have to change. Although I don't think the vandals are conscious of this.'

Oh, that was good! I really need to start writing things down!

'Really? And why's that?'

'That would require intellects capable of meaningful creation, not slogans. How could anyone growing up in a scheme nurture that? There're too many bricks.'

'You're such an arsehole.'

'Why?'

'They spray it, they mean it. They're pissed off with having nothing, being helped because they have nothing. It's obvious, you dick. Aren't you buying me a rum and coke now?'

'They may be pissed off, but their actions reverberate outside of their own understanding. What kind of rum?'

'Ha, so you're the middle class reader? Only you understand other people's words properly? And make it spiced rum.'

'At least I read. And I'm writing a novel. About porn in the future. Therapeutic pods. Can I tell you about it? Do you want ice with that?'

She's posing like a drunken teacher. I'm a foolish pupil. The women behind us click plastic things. Collective man at the fruit machine is concentrating, mumbling. Eric's in there. Families keep feeding. But why does this feel dangerous? Can see the curve of Suzie's tits though, under the Snake on her t-shirt. Nothing else has ever mattered, has it? This medication has freed me.

19

...a spokesperson stated that the family had accrued considerable debts. It is unclear whether this was a contributory factor. However, after the children's bodies were recovered from The Thames, it became clear that they had not suffered any physical abuse. The police are still conducting inquiries to locate the parents, who were seen in Devon after the discovery of the bodies.

Thank you Nigel. That was Nigel Corry with the news at 2 am. Now I have a treat for our late night listeners. Let me take you back to 1973 and the soulful sound of Roberta Flack. Enjoy...

...except I can't do that, can I? Difficult to get to the river when you're stuck above a door. How can I drown without lungs, feel cold water fill me with relief, see the calm of black without eyes, walk into water, down the steps at Curby docks, listen to the city being squeezed away without ears? I need a body to die.

Stop, it's pointless, but you've got radio, thank god he leaves it on, and this is familiar anyway, like staying awake all night, listening to John Peel, ignoring mum next door, waking, talking to herself. I had the early mornings though, no one else awake when I wandered in the violet, maybe I can see it through the window soon, can't sleep anyway, not like this. You need a body to sleep.

Wait...look, the grains are stirring, blacker ones now too, but are they black, more like sprinkles, of...dark matter, all lifting, blowing like hail, soft, in one direction, towards the window wall, faster now, and I can see something in the rush...insects, no…people shapes, walking and is that a car, think that's railings, and bushes over there? Am I in there somewhere? Can't see, it's too unfocused, too busy, like a park in a storm with black grass and trees and people in a group under black leaves, standing, with grey snow blowing through them.

Ah, it's sharper now. It's a funeral and I'm looking down at it, like I'm above, filming, look, they're smaller from here, like toys pretending to be at a funeral, but whose? I can't see faces from here, could be dad's, mum's, Ian's dad's but it can't be mum's, when Ian and I stole vodka from his dad's house, drank it in the morning, vomited in the crematorium on polished shoes, because there're no sick kids here. Auntie Jill took us to hospital, first time I had my stomach pumped and Ian bought me Salt 'n' Shake crisps. No, it can't be mum's.

It's not Dad's, there're no Spanish flags and I wasn't there so it must be Ian's dad's…no, it was dark at his, and there're too many people here for that…oh shit. There's a small coffin. Oh god. Wreaths in dolly shapes on top and I didn't pick them, best to leave these things to Kate, she's good at organising and she made chairs and bread but I can't see the faces, can't see if it's being carried by Kate's relatives, their eyes curdled with hate not for the dead, for me. But I didn't do anything. Kate, you were at work, but we should let her play outside, we agreed, didn't we, that kids need freedom, to walk, explore, find things, learn more and I built a rocket once.

Is that me down there, I *am* there then, the only one wearing a blue suit and I didn't want black, even though Kate told me she'd kill me if I didn't but she'd already tried to stab me in the kitchen. I phoned the doctor but he couldn't come out and I left after that because I could have died Kate; I had to get away from you.

Listen, birds singing because they don't know this is a funeral, do they, and cars keep driving past, the fuss never stops, so this is Curby Central Cemetery. Why did we bury her here then? Can even smell the metal of cars; hear shopper hum, even from up here and it's like everything's in a hole I'm looking into.

So where's Kate in this crater then? Oh, over there, under a tree, crying with her mum and there's the priest, saying something gently and it's raining now but I can't feel that, can I, I'm only watching. Coffin's going in and look at me, I smoke a fag and sniff, stand away from the grave, behind everybody, best that way. Oh, there's Ian, by the gate, like he's on lookout duty and Wendy died, I didn't even know, how could I? I was busy, Kate was at work, I was studying in the living room and things happen, don't they? Wendy, you're too inquisitive, sit by Daddy, draw something, I could die instead. Let me go back and die then, but that won't happen, will it? So what can I do? Nothing to do. So why all this?

Hey, there's a tiny Jan beyond the railings, in a newsagent's door like a toy spy I'd put there earlier, but thank god for Jan! I'm over there Jan, she sees me! Kate didn't want me anyway, remember, didn't want me at the funeral. I didn't kill Wendy though. But Kate's letter, she'd left it on the bed, before she moved in with her mum again, said I'd murdered our child but Jan believed me, in the pub, at her house, sometimes outside the chemist's and look, we're going away to the pub now! I'm leaving already, like I'm moving me with my giant hand, into a taxi to the Upton Arms! And no one's noticing; they're all staring into that grave. Aw, look at my cousin Ian, patting me on the back as I bend to get in the car and Kate's too busy collapsing to see, her mum's screaming. I could squash them with my finger from here but I've no hands.

It was good that I left, wasn't it? Because they all looked mad and the cars kept growling, so it was too much.

Where now? Grains swirling quicker and I'm sick. Why do I think like this, why can't I feel? I'm evil and deserve whatever this is but accidents happen, don't they? I didn't cause it, people will understand, I wasn't arrested, what can you do about it now? So where are we, a new scene…the old Upton Arms, look at its brown walls, peanuts, tobacco smoke and me, and Jan, drinking in a corner, behind a door, and I'm above them, watching, like on the nicotine ceiling.

This pub was great, wasn't it? Where old men read newspapers, drank half-pints, watched horse-racing results and I could've cried or died and they wouldn't have looked. Even the rain was older, listen to it complain on the window, like the sky has asthma and Jan's tying to tell me something about her husband, I think. He's a politician but Jan loves me, doesn't she? She doesn't have kids, has a big house and likes sex, but there's nothing wrong with that because she doesn't judge me, expect anything. It's getting dark everywhere now.

I need to stop this; I know what's going to happen. Take this away, don't want to look. Kate did this, not because of me, but because her mother was…I didn't cause it, someone must see, understand, please. I can't turn away…

Oh god, it's still there, we're sitting, our faces in dullness and Ian's there now, buying vodkas, judging the décor, why places like this are becoming extinct but it's different, seeing it this way, like we knew we were waiting for Kate to find us, why didn't we think that she'd...so there are stills in life then, moments between moments to let atoms sift and settle, the watercolour dry and here comes Kate now and the light she lets in photographs everything, that's why I can't forget. Okay, I'll look, but I'm not going to do anything about it, what can I do?

You notice her vampire eyes first, black mascara on white skin, then slits in her arms to her elbows where blood spurts escape and splash in Jan's gin. Like show and tell though, isn't it, Kate's a girl- smell the salt, see the crimson sparkle. Her mother's there too, warped, shrunk, looking for someone to stop and rewind, she tries to pull her girl away, but like a child tugging an adult, then you hear a noise from a hole inside Kate, a howl and it doesn't sound human. Old men turn from their crosswords.

Okay, I've seen it. Yes it's always been there, so what now? What can I do about this film? Can't censor, no stop button and it's still running.

Come on Ian, do something! What did you do? Oh yes, he talked to Kate, he's never told me what he said, I ran to the toilet, Jan took her gin to the bar, old men stared and Kate had gone when I returned. Only Ian there now, always Ian, he fixes things, he's speaking now, listen, he's calm, at last! Oh please say something, what did he say:

'Her mum stopped a taxi, they're off to hospital. Paul, she's really ill mate. You didn't make her ill. It wasn't your fault. You'd be better keeping your distance, isn't that right Jan.'

Here's Jan, back from the bar, that wide face, so empty, sits beside us with a bloodless gin and is this another still, a moment slowed for me to see her clean atoms slide into place as she bends into the chair, all calm and professional and what did she say?

'Yes, it's trauma, that's all. There're a host of anti-depressants to aid her recovery. She's grieving, so are you, there's nothing you can do. You need time to yourself. You both do. Wendy's death was a tragic accident.'
    'Thanks Jan.'
    'It's okay Paul.'
    'Ian, what do you really think?'
    'You really want me to say?'
    'Yeah.'

Ha, look at his face, like he's always known this would happen, his religious expression.

'Okay mate...this was inevitable. You knew this. You're not cutting your arms open, *she* is. She needs help. You know what I think?'
    'What?'
    'We should get out of here, me and you. We deserve better. I'll get a shop down south, Brighton or something.'
    'Okay.'
    'I'll check it out.'
    'Okay, Brighton it is.'

It's over. Oh thank god! Dots like sleet in slow motion, picture's stalled. It'll all stop and I'll be back in the room, with the futon and the window, nothing is changing. I can watch anything then? It's not affecting me 'cause I can't kill myself, is that it? I'm just a camera then, looking.

Something's leaving me with every show though, feeling lighter. That's okay. But why hasn't anyone noticed me, noticed *him* at work? He *must* look insane. No one ever notices me, that's why. Who would want to? It's okay, can stay like this then, there's no pain here, what's the problem? No one will miss me so bring on the films.

Something's wrong though, room's coming back but someone's there, on the futon, all misty. Who is…who the fuck is that? Oh…it's me. It's *him*.

Jesus, what've I done? Blood on his face, purple around the eyes and jaw, jacket's ripped, trousers stained, what has he done? He's attacked someone!

He'll be arrested. They'll have to do a psychological evaluation, phone my doctor, bring him in. It's almost over! But who have I, who has *he* attacked? I *knew* he would hurt someone, but I didn't know who, oh god, he's killed! It was *him* though, it wasn't *me*, that makes it different, doesn't it? Look at him, putting his ears to the wall. I'm up here, you cunt! He must know I'm here. Now he's banging on the wall, punching. An animal, he's not me, he's not me, I swear.

20

…What happened? Time is it? Why do I leave that radio on all the time? Stand up. No, get to the toilet, quick!

Phew! Where's this blood come from? Is this my face? Jesus, my side! Was I run over? Who was I with last night? Suzie! Did she do this? Why would she? What did we do then? Did we fuck? Hope we fucked. But that wouldn't cause this, would it?

Phone Ian. No, go to his house. Taxi to Fairfields. Need to sort this out. He'll laugh. That's alright.

So who's in my living room wall then? A murderous dwarf, a crying child, my soul? Doctor's trying to manipulate me. There's nothing in there! Can't hear anything. Feels the same. If anything's listening, watching, what would they hear anyway? What would they see? Nothing happens here. Need to make things happen. It's up to me. What did I do last night? Get dressed, dump the clothes, in case of…get to Ian's, stop this you cunt. Go!

Fairfields in the dream between night and day. I like that, sounded good. Should start carrying a notebook, writing things down. It's important. Listen…to this silence. There're no dramas; it's too early. Tenements are smudged. Streets softened. No shouting from behind vertical blinds. All black squares. When they wake, their faces crease with new tragedies every day.

Place looks historic like this. Or foreign, Spanish, Aztec or something.

Someone's walking behind me. Who is it…nobody. Flash of yellow in purple privet hedge, that's all.

Hard to see the bins, bus stops, pavements, dog shit. Spaces where play parks used to stand. Glass bottles in plastic bags, needles in grass, flooded with dark. No one awake to complain.

Stayed up all night for this when I was eleven years old. Three, four nights. In summertime. To see this, feel this. No one knew. Saw another earth. Wanted to live in it. Alone.

But there's Ian's house by dirty garages, pink with changing light. Council didn't plan for colour. There'll be a tax. Hate this *system*. This is the only free time, before humans wake and 'issues' choke us. Hope Ian's awake though. Knock on the door then, come on!

'Jesus Christ Paul, it's four in the fuckin' morning!'
   'Yeah, but let me in, something's happened.'
   'Get in, you crazy cunt.'

Shit, Mandy's awake. Sitting in the kitchen, smoking. Kettle's boiling. Her face's crunched. Flaking make-up. Blonde perm like a clown's wig. Pink cotton dressing gown, barmaid breasts. Pockets with holes in corners. Fag packet and lighter in her shiny hand. Painted toenails. Instantly real. Boring. I told him.

'Sit in the livingroom, Paul. I'll bring coffee.'
   'Okay.'

She'll be whispering to Ian in the kitchen. I met her in the Upton Arms. Ian's idea. Best to meet her over a drink, he said. I arrived early. Mandy and Ian were already there. Laughed when I saw her. Automatic. She was wearing a low-cut black top and a red satin bow. A fuckin' bow, where her tits disappeared into her top. I twisted my outburst into an exclamation of how glad I was to meet her. Ian's told me *so* much about you, all good. She believed me.

We moved to another table. She wanted to sit beside the juke box. I love music, she said. Want to start my own business, like Ian. Want to get a business management HND. Grinned like a magician's assistant until I asked her if she'd ever been an extra in a soap-opera. She threw her half-pint of blackcurrant and vodka over me.

She never listens to music. Ian told me. Hasn't got a business, HND, fuck all. Another human going nowhere. I told him. She wants comfort, that's it. Ian's doomed.

She made him decorate this livingroom. Black and silver wallpaper. Black leather settee. Laminate flooring. Brass fan on the ceiling. White rug. Oh, there're shadows moving across it. Human shaped. That's new. Okay, don't freak; it's the meds. Hopefully. Where's Ian?

'Here, take your coffee. Jesus Christ Paul, are you in…what do you call it…that mania thing again?'

'No, it's not like that.'

'It looks like it, mate. What's happened then? Mandy's pissed off. It's early. I'm always awake, but Mandy's…'

'Mandy…*I told you, she'll keep you down. She only wants all of this…domestic shit.*'

'Hey, come on Paul, you're wrong about her. In fact, Mandy's just been accepted for a Social Work degree at Curby University.'

'Right, fuck off.'

'Anyway, we've reached an understanding.'

'And what's that?'

Another one of his smiles. This one means he's humouring me.

'Paul, I'll tell you, but no bizarre reactions, okay? It's too early in the morning.'
'Tell me.'
'Right. Karl's left school, going to study at college part-time. I've agreed to give him some hours in the shop. Once he moves on, and Mandy graduates, Mandy and I can invest in a new project.'
'You're forty-five. Why is this a good idea?'
'I can sell up and move at forty-nine!'
'You're making excuses, like her!'
'Calm down Paul. The meds not working then? What's happened to you? Got yourself pissed, in a fight like last summer?'

Why did I come here? He never listens. Last summer was his fault. Asked him to fund my Etch-a-Sketch idea. Loan me money to buy them. So I could write a visual story with one hundred Etch-a-Sketch panels on a wall. Approached McLean Galleries with the idea. They offered me space for hire, for one week. It would have been a pastiche of digital television. I phoned the press, arranged everything. He wouldn't give me the money. I only had one Etch-a-Sketch. I wrote 'wanker' on it and left it lying against the door of Ian's shop one night. Then I got into a fight in a theme pub, its opening night, everyone was dressed as James Bond and I punched a bald man with a fake cat. Better say something, then leave.

'I can't remember. I was with a woman, that's all I can…'

'A woman…and you're in this state? Oh Paul, this doesn't look good mate, oh my god.'

'Ian, don't, come on! I can't remember anything!'

'I hope you haven't…you'd be best taking a sicky off work. A week or something.'

'What do you mean? Fucksake Ian!'

'Calm down, Paul! I only mean…keep reading the papers. Stay at home, get back to the doctors. You're needing to get off these meds mate.'

'You're not helping.'

'What do you want me to say? I don't know what happened. Maybe you were jumped by a few blokes. You're a pain when you're pissed. And you're an ugly bastard.'

'Yeah, that's it! I need to go.'

'Why?'

'Don't feel great, need a walk.'

'Fair enough.'

Who's that over there? Walking behind Ian, by the door! Oh god! Can Ian see him, he's not looking! Who the fuck, it's too dark in here, I can't…Oh, it's Karl. Why's he looking at me like that? Is he looking at me? Can't see his eyes through his hair. Wish he'd stop stooping like he's mocking some disease that means he can't talk or do anything else. He's regressing, into another research participant from Fairfields. But can't see him properly! Leave then, now!

'Right Ian, I'll get going, need that walk, try and remember last night.'

'Okay, take it easy cousin. You coming down to the shop before work?'

'No, not today. Bye.'

Mandy. She's at the door there. Leaning against its

frame. Have to pass her. Shit. She's looking at me, and I'll start writing when I finish work today but her eyes are loose, sliding around her face. One eye's domestic, tired, so that's typical, okay, breathe, what about my novel but the other is floating and sympathetic, like a hospital visitor's. Fuck! She can't be real, she can't feel, I've got to go!

Breathe, come on! Look over there at something. Yes, the post office's opened, next to Jan's chemist's. Light from the window's interesting, yes, looks Victorian like that. Like the owners: an old bald woman who wears summer dresses all year, that's right: Alice in Wonderland with an ageing disease. Her husband wears a post office blazer, a moustache, doesn't he, has trouble breathing. They've always been here. Had no children. Never left. Probably die here. This is hell!

Mail being delivered. People talking in there. Same words they always say. Shots of gold across the shop front, dissolving. Blobs of darkness on the pavement. But that's me, isn't it, so that's okay. Ignore it. Stand here, watch then, wait for Jan to open the chemist's. Remember...

Suzie. Wonderful tits. Alternative woman. Not like Jan or Christine. Depressing though. Yeah but what happened? Drinking, yes. Families, Upton Arms, meals, lights, greed, adults with money. Who else? No one. Nothing.

Keep moving then. Phone Jan later. Others moving here now. Don't want to be here. Man over there in white overalls. Paint stained boots. Flask and sandwiches in his backpack, probably. Why's he looking at me like that? I haven't done anything. What have I done? How could he know anyway? Is he looking at me? Is his face there? He's looking this way, but where's his fucking face? Oh my god! Space, a hole, where his face should…No, it's still dark, that's all, shades changing shapes. They can do that, can't they? Okay, it's a hallucination, one-fifth of patients with bipolar disorder experience hallucinations, that's what I read but I don't need to do this anymore. So let's get downtown. Buy coffee, plenty of coffee, before the library. Kill yourself…no, wait, that shouldn't have happened.

21

Why did I get coffee? Burning through the cardboard! Throw it away! Students staring at me. I'm standing behind a tree, what's the problem with that? There're too many of them. Can't focus on a face. Lime strip across them. Hairs of silver in the air. Some black shredding around me. This isn't good. Look at the grass then, at your feet. Sloppy and grey. There's Christine, opening the library doors! Oh thank god! Here I come, Christine, I'm over here, I love you, god, I really do! I love you *so* much! Come on! Barge through the bastards, that's it.

'Paul, oh my god, what's wrong?'

'Nothing, everything's *brilliant* Christine, god yeah, I've got plans!'

Tried to get Kate to give me money to self-publish a selection of short stories. Planned to launch in Borders store down by Curby docks. Did artwork for the book sleeve with crayons. Picture of a man looking in a mirror. First story would have been about a man who only spoke with his reflection. Showed it to Kate, let her read over a few paragraphs, I did, I loved her but she said it was contrived, didn't she, then went quiet. I didn't write anything else. Everything is always blocked. I need to get away.

'Paul, relax, you look…what's going on?'

'Nothing, nothing at all…were you sick last night?'

'Sick…why, do I look…what do you mean, Paul?'

'You forgot. The library was vandalised again then?'

'Come inside, Paul; we're blocking the entrance.

What did I forget?'

'You said you'd meet me last night. Upton Arms. I was there. Waited for hours.'

'Paul, I feel that…let's go into the staff room and…'

'You said you would.'

'I don't recall agreeing to meet you at all, when did…'

'What?'

'You don't look well. Have you slept at…?'

'I must have. But why's that relevant?'

She's starting to digress. They all do.

'You're face is bruised. Paul, what's happened to…?'

'I don't know. If you were there, you'd know.'

'Paul, I did not agree to meet you anywhere. I remember you mentioning something, but…'

It's hot. Too hot in here. So quickly, the heat, how did…she'd better start listening. Listening to me. Why's she not listening? Fuck! How can I get out of myself? Run out of my body? Fuck this body! Doctor said something. No. Come on! Oh look at her tits, fuck, fuck, *fuck*!

'Christine, I need to tell you about…come over here. Where it's cooler, come on.'

'God, let go of me!'

'Sorry, stress, that's all, didn't mean…please listen to me.'

'What is it?!'

'I'm leaving. Got serious plans. Not like this shit. Ideas, you know. Brighton! God, think about it, Brighton!'

'What about…'

'Writing a novel, the library down there, Ian's

getting a shop!'

'I don't understa…'

'I'm going soon. Making arrangements. Doing it for us all! Yes! Think about it!'

'Doing what? What are…?'

'No one else will. Has to be me. Always has. No one else would. No one can. Come with me. That's it. I've said it now.'

'Come with you where? To do what?'

Oh god! She's squinting! Shouldn't do that. Hate that strip light above her head. Stained. Old. Brown. Hissing. Fuck her. Fuck this job!

'Paul, please, come with me.'

'What for?'

'I'm worried ab…'

'You're nothing to me.'

'What? Now I…'

'Now you listen.'

'Yes, I…'

'Nothing here now. Can't listen to you anymore. You lied to me.'

'I've *never* lied to you! Don't you…'

'What? I *do* everything. You'll stay here. Never move. Death, it's like death. I'm not going to die!'

'Paul, come back! Paul!'

Where now? Where am I? Oh yeah. Breathe. Stand here for a bit then. You'll be alright. Everything's okay. Look at Compton Bridge. Beautiful, isn't it, reflecting waves like that, and sky, and graffiti on a concrete leg, can't read it from here. Dock area's nice though, isn't it? Look, council's done well. Listen, I'm being mindful, I am 'in-the- moment', remember doctor, we tried that. Oh and there's been refurbishment here. A new cycle path, wall and water, the bridge. It's all ornamental though, isn't it?

Ian did the right thing renting a shop here though, aw Ian. There're possibilities here, that's what it is, newness attracts people. God, look at the water! Cleaner than it used to be. Council funding, green flag, brilliant!

Jump in then. Do it! You're a killer. You killed someone last night, must have. No, you're a rapist. Could happen to anyone though, couldn't it?

Stop! Intrusive thoughts, that's all. Come on now, stop shaking.

Good. So it's Brighton then. Named Brightonhelmston by a Saxon Bishop called St. Brighthelm before changing names throughout its history. I'll pack tomorrow. Rent a flat in Kemp Town Estate. Two bedrooms. Regency residence. Sea views. Work in University of Brighton library. Apply for part-funding for a masters. Pay the rest with my wages. Oh, that should feel colder, but it's not.

After the masters, work full-time in library. Release first collection of short stories by January 2010. It'll be titled 'Stories from Your Mirror'. Published by Otter Books. £16.99. Now it's getting colder. Feet are numbing,

Organise notes for first novel within first year in Brighton. After short story publication, accept a PhD research grant on creative writing. Write first novel, go back to part-time work in library. Begin teaching undergraduates at another university. Meet a poet and start a fulfilling relationship based on artistic vitality and sex. Legs are burning with cold.

Use money from short story collection to invest in

Ian's Brighton store. Create a chain of stores. Profits allow full-time writing. Complete PhD and publish first novel in December 2010, Otter Books, £7.99. It will be called 'Letters from Hell' and will be a fictional account of someone with bipolar disorder describing his life through a series of letters written to himself. Buy a four bedroom home in Seaview on the Isle of Wight, a five minute walk from Seagrove Bay. Drink more. Write a trilogy based on confessions of ghosts. Win the Booker Prize in 2012 and in my speech thank no one. God, my legs!

'Paul!'

Who is that?

'Paul, get out of the fuckin' water! What are you doing?'

'Oh, hi Ian. I must have fallen in.'

'Get out of there! God, I can't deal with you anymore! I can't open my eyes in the morning; I can't open my shop without seeing you trying to…'

'I fell in, it's not a problem. I'm climbing out now, see?'

'You were trying to kill yourself! Why did I stop you? You've lost it! Get out of there! I'll phone the doctor!'

'Ian, I was thinking, that's all. I know what I'm doing. This isn't what it looks like. I've been making plans, for Brighton'

'I'm not going anywhere with you! Have you read the Curby Gazette yet? You're all over it, you've been named! What have you done now, you crazy bastard?'

'Nothing, I don't know what you…it wasn't me, Ian! I can't remember!'

A taxi's coming. Flag it down. Run! Where to, where now?! Here it is, get in, Ian's following, shouting something.

'Right, where to mate?'

'Ah…Curby Health Promotion, in Fairfields.'

'Are you wet, mate?'

'Only a little. I'll give you fifty pounds.'

'Right you are then. Hey, have you heard these mixed CDs mate, they're…'

22

'…so my mate downloaded them for me. Listen to this, the CD starts with Stand by Me, you know, that one the guy did in the 60s, then onto Suicide, that one from last year, but the bass line and drums are sort of the same in the mix, you know. It's like loads of songs on one track. Amazing, eh?

Oh, and listen to this one mate. It starts with Twist and Shout, then it…'

I'm in the paper. How did that happen? Be arrested soon then. Have to escape. Been in the paper before though. Two years ago. Standing at a bus stop. Bus approached. Looked in a window while lighting a fag. In one, an old man was checking the pulse of a very white child. A boy, maybe six years old. Boy's face was wet, stuck to the glass. My hand drifted, still pressed down on the lighter. Set fire to a woman's hair. She was standing next to me. Headline was about the asthma attack, heroics of old man on the bus. I was under the paragraph entitled 'witness injured'. Didn't mention her perm.

'….yeah, so on this CD it goes from The Beatles to that Mexican outfit, you know. It's amazing. Listen, I could download this stuff easy. If you like mate, leave your number, I'll pass some on. Sometimes it's like six songs on one mix. Anyway, Curby Health Promotions, was it? We're here. That'll be £50 mate.'

Why did I ask the driver to bring me here? Why did it get foggy so quickly? What happened to my…oh yeah, that's why they're wet. Ian could never understand. He's a hypocrite. Talks but doesn't act. A futureless man. It's time to quit. Go home. Wreck the flat. Burn clothes. Pack. Leave. And where am I going? Brighton, wasn't it? Don't I have to buy CDs though, six songs in one? I have to leave my number with the driver. Stop it! Get in, tell them you're leaving. Come on!

Is it raining in here? Grey lines slicing through everything! Can hardly see Frank sitting there. Is he smiling? What is...here comes Pete. Oh my god! He's washed his hair! Ironed his clothes. Even shaved! This is wrong. Why's he standing in front of Frank like that? He's putting his hands on Frank's shoulders, stopping him from standing up. What's going...oh, he's coughed.

'Stay calm, Frank. I'll talk to Paul outside. You stay here. It's not worth it, mate.'
    'Pete, what are you doing? What's wrong?'
    'Come with me, Paul.'

Look at Pete's face! It's not sucked into his neck. And he can evoke an emotion apart from disgust. Looks like sympathy. For who though? He's waving his hands, for me to follow him. Is he trying to act officious? No, not that. Confident then? Even the black trailers his hands leave are smooth. Like he's smudging charcoal air.

'Paul, come outside. Don't talk to Frank, he's raging.'
    'Raging? What about? And congratulations on overcoming your personal hygiene issues.'
    'What?'
    'Have you had your eyebrows waxed?'
    'How did you get wet? Your eyes are all over the fuckin' place.'
    'I'm concentrating. Damp trousers help. This is a very exciting time for me. Being methodological in my

planning. What are you trying to say Pete?'

'You've ruined everything. It's in the paper. Frank's going nuts. I could ask why. Maybe you're addicted to sex; maybe you've got a problem. The research is screwed. MEP saw the film. You're bipolar, aren't you? Are you manic now or are…'

Diagnosed late though. Sufferers usually categorised in late adolescence or in their 20s. Kate asked me to get an appointment after crying for two days. Talked to a shy GP with club feet. She referred me to my doctor. He diagnosed me after two interviews. I asked him if the post had been filled. Gave me handouts to read. And the mood diary sheets.

First handout was a webpage printout. A pamphlet. No, a page from a book. Listed the diagnostic criteria. Read it as I walked. Person must have one manic or hypomanic episode: not sleeping, racing thought, easily distracted, goal-orientated, found myself standing outside a caravan park by the last sentence. I'd never been there before. Must have taken a wrong turn. Where am I now? Oh yeah.

'Yes, I'm bipolar. Is this conversation going anywhere?'

'I've filled in a holiday request sheet. Sign it. I'll take it back to...'

'I can't waste time. Interview in Brighton to make tomorrow morning.'

'What? Frank wants to fire you. He's done so much for you, you cunt. He supported you when others wanted you out, you stupid fuck! I'm telling you so you can...'

'Bought a regency flat in Brighton. Got a job in Brighton University. Got an interview with Acorn Publishing. But you can't be my novel's hero anymore;

you're too clean now.'

'What? Why don't you just fuck off then?'

'In this fog?'

The caravan! Go now! Run! But I didn't think that, did I? Intrusive thought then. Ignore it. But my legs are walking. Moving without feeling. How can that happen? Pete will stop me. No he won't. There's the cleaner beside him. They're whispering. Working class solidarity. Evil union. Look, they're eyes are black now, standing at the door smoking, and I'm crossing the road away from them. Get a bus. Stop a taxi. Can't see anything though and there's Frank standing at the door with them all now. Oh god, why's his mouth like that? It doesn't look right; it's too long and black. What's in it? Where are his eyes, oh god! I liked his religious eyes, but this is…Turn the corner. Run!

Fairfields in fog. Shouts from blanked-out flats up there. Rap music warping through wet air. Shadows, things with ghost dogs and mumbles from no one and the mist is cooling my legs and there's colour trying to cut through from some windows. Slits of blues, oranges, but dissolving into grains as they die in this cloud on the ground.

Want to be lost. I'll end up in Brighton anyway. It's a natural pull. Can wander here though and I'll reach countryside, then my caravan. Rest there. Leave for the station in the morning. Arrange notes for the short-story collection tonight. A portfolio of ideas. Write an abstract, one paragraph linking each story in theme. Stories of being trapped in human bodies. Then masturbate, sleep, die. No, no death.

There must be a road somewhere that leads to the fields and what's happened to the earth? Am I still walking on it? Is this another dimension, of grey, with

colour dots like bees in a cloudy bush and I can't feel
or see my feet or anything else? I've slipped out of
myself and birds are screaming and I don't want to go
back to hospital, please no! It's only a buzzing and it's
itchy inside my head and I know what it means. I can
walk in this cotton world though, it's okay, don't have
any feeling anyway, no one will look for me. The
planet's covered now, forever, and Jan and Penny will
wander, holding hands, looking for lost husbands to
fool and Frank will grope to find the disadvantaged
with Pete looking for Frank to tell him something
important and Ian will sit still with Mandy and Karl in a
puddle by a road, waiting for something to happen but
it's better like this because it's not the end, is it? Faces
swirling in the fog and I know they're not real, that's
the difference, didn't someone say something on a
handout?

Look! Is that real? It must be! A wall, over there. And a
sign…it's…Bourne Caravan Park! This proves that I'm
not a human like them! No one can do this, to loose
yourself in nothing and find home. That's where I am
now, home. Can live here until the buzzing goes. I can
do *any*thing. Then I'll have a full manuscript to take to
Brighton. Show an editor at Otter Books. No
photograph on the back sleeve though. No story about
the author. How he returned from hospitalisation to
work and write a novel based on the adventures of a
transvestite manic depressive. How his every action
was heroic as he pushed through a haze of medication
and stigma to create. No, that's not a story worth
reading and here's my caravan and I know the other
caravans are here somewhere and I'll write 'Paul
Belardo exists' on the inner sleeve.
  Someone's sprayed 'FUCK HO…' across the wall
of the park entrance, they must have been disturbed

131

mid-spray and there's a shit stain on the organic looking bricks, and burnt newspapers on the grass. Bastards are even attacking caravan parks! I've got to escape this! It's all been directed at me! The campaign, it's been around me, I knew it, the bastards must know me, knew that I would want to die when being terrorised by the mundane, they know I'll die now, but how? Have I brought medication with me? There's the caravan there, open the door, come on! Walk in. Nothing. Looks the same. Two chairs. One radio. A table with books from the second hand shop in Upton Mews. A cigarette packet filled with bee remains, lying on the floor. The sink, microwave. Fold-down bed, naked lamp. Empty vodka bottle, box of tissues.

Sit down, stop shaking. There. Let the rushes zip over your head. Leave it, it's okay. Safe here, aren't we? What did I do though? They'll jail me in a hospital but what if I stay here? That's fair, isn't it? I won't do anything and the air in here is brown now. Stop jerking and close your eyes and wait and write tomorrow, maybe the story of my Wendy and the wire. Switch the radio on. That's better.

23

'And is this causing you to feel this way, Margaret?'

'Yes...yes, I think so, Wayne. Things have been a disaster since he left.'

'Why do you think he left, Margaret? Is it okay to ask this?'

'Yes...yes, it's okay. I think I became unattractive to him. I was concentrating so much on getting our bakery business running, I didn't think of myself anymore. I didn't think of him anymore. Oh god, I took it all for granted Wayne!'

'That's okay, Margaret. And how many paracetamol tablets have you taken this evening, Margaret?'

'About twenty, I think. I'm so sorry for being such a pain.'

'It's okay Margaret. Please, stay on the line and we'll get you help right away.'

Well, ladies and gentlemen, we'll have to stop there, I'm afraid. But Wayne will be back next week for his regular phone-in session. The Samaritans play such a vital role in our communities, don't they?

Okay, well, that leaves us with enough time for one more track before the news. It's back to 1980 now with a Neil Diamond classic...

How did that happen? Didn't feel the drop but I'm above the floor and don't know what day and night is anymore, so I'm floating? Can I turn around? No. Feel the current though, metal pepper ripping through, jagged, loud now inside, yes, sounds like mist on pylons, doesn't it, these atoms in psychosis hissing.

But the wall, all dulled, unfamiliar, spaces there, of…nothing. Not blackness though, is it, more…a lack of matter, yeah, gaps, I've seen them before, when I was tricking sleep in bed when I was young, seen them on the roof, the door.

And over there, under the window, holes, and an iron sky outside, dimpled with void! What's happening? How can I see anything in bits then? Where will the shows run? Look to the left, plenty of wall still there, grains louder already, like a crowd, feel their surge; I'm in a black wave, part of it, we're rising like vomit, flu in motion, these atoms are ill. I feel like a virus, not human and why hasn't *he* been arrested yet, is everyone *blind*?

We're all dancing, I'm a bouncing germ, ha, but there's no logic to this, is there, like a sneeze on a bus, everything's splitting, congealing, over there, lumps of colour and now I'm here…wow, I didn't even feel that. That was the quickest yet. When am I? Look then. Oh my god!

Must be the seventies, maybe 76? There's mum sitting at the dinner table with brown tiles on top, the only new thing she ever bought, even polished it once, aw, and a dying cheese plant behind her, dad sitting to her left, with her cigarette cards, making professional piles, tying them with elastic bands, oh dad. Am I sitting at this table? Must be. Look down; my hands are there, child hands, playing with little soldiers in a blur. Wow, I'm *inside* the film this time! The camera must be behind my eyes then!

Ha, mum, her face, stopped looking before she died, but can look now, it's alright, can see that she's chewing a cringe, evil and a new perm because maybe she's a little better this week son but dad ignores everything, doesn't he, sits there, writing things, touching things, making noises to show he exists, nothing, but I can look.

What's outside, in the garden? I'm really in this one! Better than watching from up there, isn't it, and air's whispering the orange curtains apart, I feel it, and you can see out, summer's a big space but it's only yellow grass, high, nasty and that greenhouse of mould and lime where I dreamed of falling into myself and forgetting who I was but why am I here? What happened? Our sixth home in the city, ground floor flat with a garden behind an old hotel called 'Curby Towers'.

Wait. This is when…hah! Look at mum and dad, you'll see, no, between them, in the middle there. Is it there yet? No? Wait…here it comes, a depression in the air, blue and black, sinking into somewhere I don't know, grains or insects or something buzzing around its edge, my first vision, told the doctor, said it was like a hole but he didn't believe me, said I was too young, but here it is, probably always been there. Tell mum then.

'Mum, what's that black thing beside you?'

'Nothing.'

Look at dad instead. His ironed arms are softening, getting ready to drift into the hole beside him, atom by atom and I can see his eyes, with nothing to cling to inside, wet with pretending to me and try to understand that mum has to sleep sometimes and she doesn't mean it when she shouts at me and you, everything will be fine if we're quiet and I always knew you were lying and ready for this hole that's whirling now and look, your arms are dissolving.

She knows that space is taking her. Her mouth's shifting, liquorice gums, eyes fading into that fairground inside her, where she lives, dad told me once, good to think of it in this way, like I did then, her always riding on waltzers made of wind, where she

135

laughs about us, but it wasn't her fault, was it?

Dad, what are you doing now, snapping an elastic band around the cigarette tokens to give us a normal sound, you do that a lot and now you're making tea and humming something in Spanish so you were nothing, but you were there, that's all you were, just there, some cloudy dad in threatened air and this is when I knew I could do anything, didn't need anyone.

But who's in the kitchen there? That noise, no one ever came, only Philippe and Ian, doctors sometimes but someone's shaking the wall, from the other side, shocking the photographs of mum, dad, me as a baby all outside Curby Central Museum, beside a statue of Gladstone and photos aren't real, are they, they're only a picture for stories we make later that have never been true but everything's trembling, the whole room and mum and dad have stopped, parts of them missing, like I'm inside a photograph that's been rubbed for too long, but this one's real because I'm taking it.

What was that...a flash. Jesus! Where's the kitchen wall gone? Sunshine, sky there, an older blue though, is that next door...no, it's another garden, we're in another film, that was instant...it's the back garden of Barnaby Cottage! Mud, barbed wire fence, an empty rabbit's hutch and...oh no, Wendy's legs, below me, her perfect white legs, with blood dots. Have to get away, come on! Stop the film! Stop right here!

I'll take anything instead of this. Oh god. There're daisies there, at her feet, oh god please, they're stained too, and her little maroon skirt and black patent leather shoes and pink socks but she must've taken them off. Can smell hogweed from the stream, maybe she wanted to explore, always exploring Wendy, weren't you, but how did this happen? Someone will come soon Wendy, where's Kate? I told her not to leave us, I did Wendy!

I'll stay with you then and hear the tractor Wendy, puffing in the fields of yellow flowers and it's summertime and there're bees, remember the bee you found, dying, died in your hand and you cried and we buried it in an empty cigarette packet, remember, and listen, a fair's in the village with tea-cup rides, hear the children and mums and dads laughing, please? So this was it, you hung here, like this, from the fence, my little girl, did you? I'll wait with you, how can I free you, doesn't matter what I do though, what do you want me to do? I, no *he* won't leave Shelley and Coleridge, he must be sitting in the cottage now, reading but I had to do it, *he* had to do it, for us, because we have to make sacrifices, darling.

Look, your eyes are the same, your nursery eyes, your Christmas eyes, wet, amazed, looking at me now but they're still, that's all, doesn't mean anything, does it? They look like marbles and I painted the door handles silver for you, your favourite colour and where's Kate? Why did this happen? Your skin is yellow like poison and I can't do anything, Wendy, can't we just wait here then, I think you're trying to smile, smile at Daddy?

That's it! Yes, stand up! Come on now, that's *it* sweetie! Oh you're such a clever girl, aren't you, yes, come to Daddy, that's it darling, oh look at you, all blood and smiles now, what a mess, you're so naughty and what are you trying to say? Oh, you can't speak; you've got a sore throat, come with Daddy then, we'll get the wire out honey, this way, and Daddy will tell you all about barbed wire and that's it, hold my hand, let's go inside and barbed wire was used a long time ago darling, to keep out Indians, and bandits, from the cowboy ranches with all the cows, in America, remember I told you? Cows moo, that's right and there were lots of barbed wire fences, with funny names like Open Diamond and Knife Edge, I know you're trying to laugh.

This way darling, into the kitchen, I'll get you a drink of water, your other daddy will be reading next door but I'm your real daddy and I'm here, so don't worry. Drink this, that's it, now let me wipe your face, get you clean for mummy getting back and sit on my knee now, that's it. She'll be *so* happy to see you, can you hear the children laughing in the village, there must be rides and let me tell you all about fairs.

Upton Mews has had fairs for a long time honey, like two hundred years, isn't that amazing, and long ago there were big games with people who would come from other villages that aren't here anymore, *huge* games that were like football and funny dances and things with flowers and songs and you smell of flowers. And people would dress up in funny clothes, yeah! They have tea-cup rides now and big swings and it's sunny outside and will we go when mummy gets back? Yeah? No sweeties though. What are you pointing at, honey? Tell daddy…oh that's right, you've got a sore throat. Well you point, and daddy will follow. Oh I'm going to be a great dad, Wendy! What, through here, you want me to follow you here? But what's here, honey, it's all dark? Hold my hand. Wendy! Hold

my

hand

please

I can't

where are you…

where am I…

Please let this be it…

…smell of…piss…Wendy, have you…*oh*. I'm *breathing*. I can turn my head! Yes! Can I touch anything? What about that cigarette packet on the floor? Look! I'm picking it up! Rattling it! Dead bees must be inside but what floor is this? There's a fold-down bed and I'm alive, oh my god, I must be! Stand up and…oh no, bad idea, sit down, you're moving too fast then. Have a look around, breath in this old air, let some blood reach these fucking cold legs. There's a sink, microwave, table and this is the caravan then! How did I get here? Does it matter though and what am I wearing? I can't see.

Feels like something heavy on my arms. Yes, these are *my* arms, not *his* and why are they so glued to the floor then? Something's pulling them down. Try lifting them up. No, that won't work. But hey, you're back, it's over! This is shock, that's all, it'll pass. So sit, *phew*, we're on holiday, yeah, it's the caravan and I love the sound of rain on the dirty window on the roof. Hear it, like a liquid mantra. I saw my little girl. Wendy.

This is it. This is the start of something. I can do anything now. I always have been able to do anything. I'll speak to Ian; sure he mentioned something about another shop in Brighton. I can help him, maybe Jan will join us. Or Christine. Can stay here for a while though, with the smell of dead bees and alcohol, a religious smell, no one would get it. But this *is* godly, god would be proud; this darkness is like a blanket from god. I'm alone but victorious, I can forgive anybody, I can suffer and survive. I'm being rewarded; I've made it. Everyone else has gone!

Pain! Ha, I'd forgotten! Where is the pain? In my chest here, in the middle. And a weakness in the arms. Warm shock in the wrists, but it's blissful, is that right? And this relief, it's spiritual, but I don't know why. Dizzy too, but they're only human things. To be human is to have symptoms, isn't it? But don't sleep, it might happen again. I'm back; there will be no return to *that*. I have to write it all down! My first novel! A book about a bipolar patient enduring prolonged psychosis! An original voice; fragmented narrative, modernist time frame, gothic influences. That's it! There's a notebook under the table. Get up! No, crawl to it!

Ah, what's this stuff on the floor? Syrup? It's a bit dark though. Wendy liked syrup. Ate it on pancakes for supper, sometimes on waffles for lunch, after a soft boiled egg with soldiers, her fingerprints in the butter. And she liked making chocolate cakes with cereal with her mum, saw them together once with a big glass bowl and sticky smiles under a yellow light in the kitchen. But Wendy's okay now, isn't she, that's what it all means, doesn't it?

What *is* this? Thick, sick, over my hands. Salt and

vomit smell. Ah. It's...blood. But whose? Did I, did *he*...oh...he did. Can see the cut, tiny but precise, it takes practice. But why? This is *my* fucking body! The cunt! A suicide, without consent, murdering bastard! God how long have I been bleeding? I've murdered myself! But this isn't my blood, it's his! Why should I...

What's that, there, a light. A reflection? From where? Look, up at the window! It's torchlight! Aw look at it, darting around like pure energy, lost. And voices! Listen to that, is that Ian outside, and Jan? It must be!

Yes, and Wendy's fine now! I'll tell Ian, he'll be pleased. See, *everything's* fine now. Yes! I'll survive. This is not my end, it's...my character's, in my book! Yes, that's it! Shit, I need to start now! Still got notes from the doctor, photocopies, so no need for research. Will they let me write in the hospital? I'll explain that this was a mistake. I was on a trial, that's all. This novel will fall onto the pages! I'll leave Curby Health Promotion, continue on at the library, write during the afternoons, meet Jan at weekends, date Christine. And I'll be published in a year! That's it! It'll have a black cover, glossy, but no photo, and no blurb apart from 'I LIVE'.

And how will it start? A description, yes, an argument, with myself, about what to call this, like hiding under myself or something. No, that's stupid. Or it's like being lost in fog, all the time. Not bad. Or it's like I'm already dead, and...no...

Bibliography

Wilde, O., 1992. *The Picture of Dorian Gray.*
Hertfordshire: Wordsworth Editions Limited.

Lightning Source UK Ltd.
Milton Keynes UK
UKOW041818260513

211266UK00002B/21/P